A Vow of Poverty

A Vow of Poverty

VERONICA BLACK

St. Martin's Press
New York

Library of Congress Cataloging-in-Publication
Data

Black, Veronica.
A vow of poverty / by Veronica Black.
p.   cm.
ISBN 0-312-14756-2
I. Title.
PR6052.L335V69   1996
823'.914—dc20   96-25531   CIP

First published in Great Britain by Robert Hale
Limited

First U.S. Edition: November 1996

10   9   8   7   6   5   4   3   2   1

A Vow of
Poverty

One

Mother Dorothy, Prioress of the Cornwall House in the Order of the Daughters of Compassion, sat at her flat-topped desk and, from behind her wire-rimmed spectacles, let her eyes sweep the semicircle of nuns ranged before her. The room in which they sat had been the elegant drawing-room of Tarquin House but the Tarquins were gone now, had been gone for more than fifteen years, and only the delicate silk panels set into the walls, the heavy curtains of faded velvet at the huge bay window, the patina of dull gold at the moulded cornices of walls and ceiling, echoed past glories. The spindle-legged chairs and tables, the ornaments and Aubusson carpet had long since vanished into various sale rooms. Now the floor was an expanse of shining polished oak; a plain crucifix hung over the high mantelpiece with an arrangement of dried grasses in the fireless grate; there were filing cabinets ranged along one wall, her own plain desk and chair, and the stools on which the sisters sat. Mother Dorothy who was the least sentimental of women wasted no time in regretting what had gone. Tarquin House had proved a very convenient base for the Order, situated as it was on the slopes of the moor, with plenty of land and rooms of a good size that, so far, had betrayed no trace of dry rot or deathwatch beetle or any other creeping infestation that sought to destroy old buildings.

'The question,' she said in her crisp light voice, 'is one of finances.'

'Or lack of them,' Sister Perpetua said, tugging at the lock of greying red hair that strayed from beneath her veil.

'Exactly!' Mother Dorothy gave her infirmarian a brisk nod. 'As you all know the rule of our Order states that we must be self-supporting, each house being responsible for its own financial arrangements. As we're only a semi-cloistered order that means we can take suitable outside work provided it doesn't interfere with our religious life.'

'Mary Concepta and I would be only too glad to work,' Sister Gabrielle said, 'but I don't know who'd employ us.'

'Both you and Sister Mary Concepta have earned a peaceful retirement,' Mother Dorothy said.

'One does so dislike being useless,' Sister Mary Concepta said tremulously. She had once been a very pretty girl and was now a very pretty old lady, her skin still delicate, her eyes retaining more than a trace of brilliant blue. At her side Sister Gabrielle, even further along in her eighties, looked leathery and tough despite the rheumatism that knotted her joints.

'I'm sure I couldn't manage all the mending without Sister Gabrielle and Sister Mary Concepta to help me,' Sister Katherine said.

A nice child, Mother Dorothy thought, her eyes resting briefly on the younger woman's pale, fine-boned face. Sister Katherine was mistress of linen and in addition brought much needed revenue with her exquisite lacework. Next to her Sister Martha, even more small and slender, looking as if a puff of wind would blow her away, was gardener, selling off fruit and vegetables that weren't eaten in the convent. Those two earned their keep.

'I am making quite rapid progress with my books of saints for children,' Sister David piped up defensively, pushing her spectacles higher on her rabbit nose.

'I'm sure you'll find a publisher,' Mother Dorothy encouraged, 'and, of course, there is your translation work which is invaluable.'

Sister David also combined the tasks of librarian and sacristan which left her no free time at all. There remained Sister Hilaria, who as novice mistress had charge of the convent's one postulant, Bernadette, who sat, eyes downcast within the brim of her large white bonnet, booted feet peeping from beneath the hem of her pink smock. Sister Hilaria was a godly woman, highly mystical, but lacking that streak of practical good sense that would have rendered her valuable. Certainly she was not earthbound enough to hold down an ordinary job. Sister Teresa, the recently professed laysister and the novice, Sister Marie, had their hands full with the cleaning and cooking, and couldn't be spared to take on outside labour. There remained Sister Joan who sat at the end of the row looking as usual as if she was about to jump up and rush off somewhere else.

Sister Joan, Mother Dorothy reflected, was a problem. She was one of the liveliest and most talented of the community – her drawings and paintings had a vigour that struck the prioress as being too virile, too highly coloured, bordering on the unconventional. If she was allowed to paint her work would almost certainly find a market, but Mother Dorothy had always hesitated about permitting Sister Joan to use her gifts, suspecting that in the younger woman personal pride in her accomplishments was by no means dead. She also had an amazing capacity for attracting incident and excitement to her small, neat person. If Sister Joan were sent out for a country walk she was liable to be kidnapped by hijackers or stumble on a body. Mother Dorothy let a small, cold shiver pass through her frame before she spoke.

'Sister Joan could, of course, teach art but with the cuts in education local schools are cutting down their staff. And our recent attempt to establish weekend retreats had, as you all know, a most unfortunate conclusion.* I am reluctant to try that experiment so soon again. Quite apart from anything else we do need the postulancy. Sister Hilaria and Bernadette are very far from comfortable up in the storerooms.'

'Are we to return to the postulancy?' Sister Hilaria asked, clearly dragging her attention back from some dream of astral glory.

The postulancy had once been the dowerhouse where widowed Tarquin ladies were safely tucked away to live out their declining years. It had been adapted to accommodate Sister Hilaria and at least six postulants but, with the shortage of vocations, only the dark-eyed Bernadette was in Sister Hilaria's charge.

'I've been thinking what's best to do,' the prioress said. 'I believe that Sister Hilaria and Bernadette will be more

* See *Vow of Fidelity*

comfortable in the postulancy which was, after all, adapted for the purpose of lodging intending sisters in a quiet place apart from the professed members of the community, but there are spare cells there which ought to be occupied. It occurred to me that our laysister and our novice could sleep over there instead of having to make do with the two tiny cells off the kitchen. Sister Teresa and Sister Marie will move their things over later today.'

It meant they'd have to walk through the grounds to do their tasks in the main house, but both Sister Teresa and Sister Marie looked pleased.

'I fail to see how that will solve our financial problems,' Sister Perpetua said.

'Once the storerooms are free again,' Mother Dorothy said, 'we can begin to clear them.'

She noticed with a twinge of amusement that Sister Joan's dark-blue eyes immediately sparkled at the prospect of action.

'The storerooms are crammed with rubbish,' Sister David said.

'We don't know that it is all rubbish,' Mother Dorothy pointed out. 'When our Order acquired this house the property was bought as it stood with most of the contents. Whatever had been packed away was simply left. I appreciate that nothing of value was said to be there, but what wasn't of value once may come into fashion again. Toy cars from the forties, late Victorian fire-irons, that kind of thing still has a market value, I understand. We might just find something.'

'A chest of gold doubloons,' Sister Perpetua said, displaying an unexpected romantic streak.

'I doubt that,' Mother Dorothy said, 'but there may well be something worth selling, and even if there's nothing we will have acquired two large upper rooms that will enable us to extend the library if it becomes necessary. Sister Joan, I'm entrusting the task to you. Since you know something of art and that kind of thing you're not likely to throw out anything that might be saleable.'

Sister Joan's blue eyes flashed with hard-held temper. Why on earth Mother Dorothy equated art with the ability to sort out rubbish was beyond her. It looked as if she regarded the ability to paint as being commensurate with the flair for spotting a bargain!

'Sister?' Mother Dorothy looked at her.

'Yes, Mother Prioress, I shall be happy to clear out the storerooms,' Sister Joan said.

'If you need help moving anything heavy let me know,' Sister Perpetua said.

'Thank you, Sister.'

'What about Brother Cuthbert?' Sister Hilaria said.

The others looked at her.

'What about Brother Cuthbert?' Mother Dorothy enquired.

'He is here staying at the old schoolhouse on a year's sabbatical from his monastery.'

'Yes, Sister, we know that,' Sister Perpetua said.

'He's a very strong young man,' Sister Hilaria said in her vague fashion. 'And very obliging.'

'You're absolutely right, Sister!' Mother Dorothy's brow cleared. 'Brother Cuthbert would certainly come over and lend a hand if it were necessary. I'll leave it to you to decide if and when you require his help, Sister Joan.'

'Yes, Mother Prioress.' Sister Joan had shaken off her mood of ill-temper and answered with her usual brightness.

'Then I think that's it. Sister Teresa and Sister Marie will help Sister Hilaria and Bernadette to move back into the postulancy and move their own things over at the same time,' Mother Dorothy said, rising. '*Dominus vobiscum.*'

'*Et cum spiritu sancto,*' the sisters chorused back.

She watched them file out, hands clasped at waist level, eyes lowered in approved fashion and sat down again, rubbing her temples where the familiar headache had begun. Being prioress was a task she performed to the best of her ability; being prioress was a privileged position she wouldn't be sorry to lay down when elections were due in a couple of years' time.

The sisters were dispersing to their various occupations. Sister Joan stood in the wide hall with its sweeping staircase and watched them go, the two elderly nuns leaning on their sticks more heavily than they had done in the summer. A sudden fear clenched her heart. The community wouldn't be the same when Sister Gabrielle and Sister Mary Concepta were gone. She sent up a silent plea that both of them should live to be a hundred, and went across to the door which led into the chapel wing. A narrow corridor, with windows along one side, bent round the small visitors' parlour with its dividing grille towards the chapel.

The chapel was cool and silent, late dahlias drooping sleepy petals over the edge of the vase on the Lady Altar. She genuflected to the main altar and began to mount the spiral stairs that wound up to the library and storerooms above. This upper wing was closed off from the rest of the house, and at night the door leading to the chapel on the ground floor was locked. Above her she could hear the others moving about, collecting mattresses and blankets in readiness for the move back to the postulancy.

'Is that you, Sister Joan?' Sister Teresa came to the head of the staircase, a pile of towels in her arms. 'How do you think you're ever going to get any of the big stuff out of the storerooms and down the stairs? We'll have to break down the wall in order to get them into the main part of the house!'

'Which will only make more expense,' Sister Joan said practically. 'We'd do better to hoist anything we don't need out of the windows. They're large enough.'

'Well, don't try doing anything like that by yourself,' Sister Teresa said. 'Get Brother Cuthbert to help you.'

'That won't be for months,' Sister Joan said, stepping to the door of the storerooms and looking somewhat gloomily at the boxes piled almost to the ceilings, the piles of old newspapers and magazines, the broken bits of furniture. 'I'll just work my way through systematically.'

The prospect of finding anything worth selling seemed remote but at least she had a definite job and so felt less like a spare part in the community. Since the little local school where she had first taught had closed she had missed the discipline of regular paid employment. Her stint as acting lay sister had been marked by her own inability to cook properly, and cut thankfully short when Sister Teresa had made her final profession.

'Do you need any help now?' she asked.

'No, thank you, Sister. We're managing very nicely,' Sister Hilaria assured her, unmistakable relief on her large, pale face as she watched her bedding being carted down the twisting staircase on its way back to her beloved postulancy.

Sister Joan turned and went downstairs again, passing

through the chapel to the outside door which led into the rough ground surrounding the house. To her left the coarse grass became cobbles and a stableyard. Alice, the Alsatian puppy acquired as a potential guard dog, frolicked over to her, tail wagging furiously.

'Some guard dog you are!' Sister Joan said, giving her a pat. 'Come! let's take Lilith for a walk.'

The convent pony, chewing meditatively in her stable, whinnied as Sister Joan undid the latch and let her out. Normally she'd have donned the permitted jeans under her grey habit and indulged in a thundering good gallop, but the ground was soft after the recent rain, and the air muggy. A walk would have to suffice.

She looped the reins over her arm and led the pony round to the front of the main house, glancing back at the handsome façade of the building with the usual pleasure. Her own novitiate had been spent in the London House where the enclosure gardens had been shut in by the streets of the city and tranquillity hard won in the hum of the passing traffic. Here, on the moors, with the town tucked at the foot of the billows of peat and grass, and the tang of the sea borne on the wind when it gusted in the right direction, the cloistered life was easier.

She walked through the open gates onto the track that snaked towards the town five miles off, passing the old schoolhouse which, once part of the Tarquin estate, was now the property of the Order, past the path that led away towards the Romany camp. The turf was still quick with heather, its purple petals unseasonably bright. It was a close, warm winter with no snap in the yellowing leaves. Sister Perpetua had been brewing up her cough mixture of wild garlic and coltsfoot in readiness for winter influenza.

'Sister Joan! Sister Joan!'

The shout came from a loose-limbed fellow who shambled towards her, shaggy head on one side, mouth wide open.

'Hello, Luther!' Sister Joan greeted him pleasantly.

Luther was somewhat wanting in his wits, though there were times when he was as lucid as the next man. Today seemed to be one of those times. He saluted her smartly as if he'd actually been in the military and fell into step beside her.

'Padraic will have fish at the weekend,' he said.

Padraic Lee was Luther's cousin three or four times removed. He lived with a wife subject to alcoholic binges and two small daughters in a caravan he kept clean and sparkling, and regularly supplied fish to the convent, though Sister Teresa wisely didn't enquire from which river or pool it had been netted.

'Thank him, will you?' Sister Joan said.

'I was wondering if there was any work for me this month,' Luther said.

Sister Joan hesitated. Luther helped out with odd jobs at the convent in return for a good hot meal and some tobacco, but the tasks consisted mainly of helping Sister Martha load vegetables on her cart ready for market or gathering apples and pears for her. Letting him loose in the storerooms where there might be some valuable stuff might be something of a risk.

'We'll be clearing some things out of the top floor soon,' she temporized, 'so if there's anything to be carted away and sold for scrap I'll see you get the first chance.'

'Thank you, Sister.' Luther grinned at her and loped off across the moor.

Sister Joan gazed after him for a moment, reflecting how lucky he was to live as he did, without the supervision of well-meaning people who would have tagged him and categorized him and treated him like a case history instead of a person. Here, on the moor, he was simply accepted for what he was, and nobody labelled him with some euphemistic phrase that meant nothing in the real world.

'Good morning, Sister Joan! You're very thoughtful today.'

Brother Cuthbert, fresh young face shining below the flaming red hair that circled his tonsure, bounded towards her, shouting a greeting.

'Good afternoon, Brother Cuthbert,' Sister Joan said.

'Is it afternoon already?' The young friar looked surprised. 'I've been in meditation and that means I always lose track of time. You know how it is!'

'For you, perhaps, but seldom for me,' she confessed ruefully. 'When I'm trying to meditate I find my mind skips all over the place and then my stomach starts rumbling and my knees begin to ache, and the sound of the bell is sweet liberation.'

'Ah! the truly holy have no need of meditation,' Brother Cuthbert said. 'They already live a recollected life.'

'That doesn't apply to me either,' Sister Joan said, laughing. 'You have a superb way of seeing only the best in people, Brother!'

'I speak as I find, Sister,' he insisted. 'Were you coming to see me or just walking Lilith? Ah, here's Alice! Now I'd a biscuit somewhere that I meant to eat but she'll not object to sharing it with me, I hope!'

Alice was quite ready to share half a dozen biscuits and Sister Joan coaxed Lilith round to begin the homeward walk.

'I was coming over to the convent,' Brother Cuthbert said, suiting his pace to her own. 'Mother Dorothy wishes me to play for the carol service at Christmas. I said I would come over to discuss the various tunes. I think "Silent Night", don't you?'

'And, "In the Bleak Midwinter",' Sister Joan said eagerly. 'I think I love that best of them all! How odd it seems to be talking about Christmas at the beginning of November! And with the weather so muggy too!'

'I start looking forward to Christmas the minute Easter's over!' Brother Cuthbebrt admitted. 'Quite wrong of me, of course, with Corpus Christi and Whitsuntide and all the other festivals in between! Father Superior often had cause to rebuke me for wishing away the months. Oh, I had a letter from him the other day and he asked to be remembered to you.'

'That's very kind of him. Will you send him my good wishes when you reply?' Her thoughts reverted briefly to the Scottish loch on which Brother Cuthbert's monastery was situated. A strange, wild place where strange, wild events sometimes took place.*

Aloud she said, 'Do you miss it – the monastery, I mean? The peace and the silence and the isolation?'

'Yes, of course.' He looked slightly surprised at the question. 'But this year in the world and yet not of the world is doing me a lot of good! It's very easy to become a little bit selfish and insular when one only mixes with religious, you see, and then having the use of the little school as a lodging gives me a certain amount of independence too which is very nice, but I

* See *Vow of Sanctity*

do miss my companions sometimes! It's a sad weakness in me, to become attached to my friends. When I go back to Scotland next year I shall probably miss everybody here as well! People have been so extraordinarily kind to me. Any little I can do to help in return—'

'Does that include carting rubbish?' Sister Joan asked.

'From the gardens? Sister Martha had thought of having a bonfire.'

'From the storerooms. I have the task of clearing them out in the hope of finding something saleable but any heavy stuff will have to be lowered from the windows.'

'Any time you need a strong back and two willing hands, Sister,' Brother Cuthbert said promptly, 'you know where to come.'

'Thank you, Brother Cuthbert. Actually, we're rather hoping that something valuable will turn up amid all the rubbish,' she confessed. 'You know that our Order bought the estate from the Tarquin family intact, but nobody ever got round to clearing out the storerooms over the chapel wing. I daresay that in the old days the servants slept there, in three big dormitories.'

'And the family died out?'

'I believe the last of them is still alive – Grant Tarquin. We have no contact with him.'

She spoke somewhat shortly, her face clouding as she recalled her own brief acquaintanceship with the last of the Tarquins. It was an experience she preferred to forget.*

A man was emerging from the convent gates, a haversack over his shoulder, his gold ear-ring and red neckerchief proclaiming the Romany. He waved to the two approaching and quickened his pace to meet them.

'Afternoon, Sister Joan! Brother Cuthbert! I've just been having a bit of a gossip with Sister Perpetua, took her some nice trout and some wild garlic I found. Too damp for much else! Alice is getting a mite plump. She hasn't been – begging your pardon, Sister – having it off with one of my lurchers, has she?'

'She has only been in season once,' Sister Joan said, amused.

'Once is often enough,' Padraic Lee said with a wink. 'Sister

* See Vow of Silence

Perpetua says you're going to clear out the attics. Don't forget me when you're tossing scrap iron out of the windows. Anything that's no use to you load on to a skip and we'll split the profits. Can't say fairer than that, now can I?'

'Indeed you can't,' Sister Joan said, 'but it'll take weeks to clear and sort it, so don't hold your breath until Christmas.'

'With the carol service.' Padraic's lean brown face creased into a smile. 'We look forward to that, Sister.'

'And to the punch that goes round afterwards,' Sister Joan said cynically.

'That's a wicked slander, Sister!' Padraic said with a grin. 'You ought to give credit for spiritual feeling.'

'Indeed I ought, even if it only comes once or twice a year,' she agreed.

'If I came regular to mass it'd give God too much of a shock,' Padraic said. 'I make sure the children go though.'

'How are Edith and Tabitha?' Sister Joan asked.

'Right as foxes,' their father said proudly. 'They miss having you to teach them though. Edith's going on nine now and very quick, and Tabitha'll be ten soon.'

'And your wife's well?'

'She has her ups and downs,' Padraic said, a casual tone masking pain. 'She wasn't so well last month but she's a lot better now.'

Meaning that she was recovering from one of her alcoholic binges, Sister Joan thought, and reminded herself not to nag Padraic about regular attendance at mass. It was due to him that his daughters were clean and neat and well behaved.

'I'd better get on,' Padraic said, breaking the silence. 'Have you seen Luther anywhere around?'

'Earlier when I first started out.'

'Then I reckon he'll turn up sooner or later,' Padraic said in a resigned tone. 'Not that he'd harm a fly but I like to keep an eye peeled.'

He loped off, the haversack bumping against his back. Doubtless it contained other fish snatched from doubtful sources.

'A very godly man,' Brother Cuthbert observed as they started up the drive.

'Yes. Yes, I suppose that he is,' Sister Joan said, considering the remark. 'Yes, you're right as usual, Brother Cuthbert!'

'I'm generally right twice a day like a stopped clock,' Brother Cuthbert said. 'There's Mother Dorothy looking out for me and wondering why I'm strolling instead of running to her command. God bless, Sister!'

He went off towards the main door and Sister Joan led Lilith back round to the yard where she secured her in her stall, and shooed Alice into the kitchen where Sister Perpetua was cleaning and gutting a heap of plump speckled trout.

Sister Joan went round to the chapel door and let herself in. This outer door which led into the chapel passage was, by custom, left open though Detective Sergeant Mill gravely disapproved on the grounds of security.

'You may well be correct, Detective Sergeant Mill,' Mother Dorothy had said with reluctance, 'but we like to think that God's own place is always available for anyone, night or day, who feels the need of prayer. We do, of course, follow your advice and lock the connecting door to the enclosure but beyond that I'm really not prepared to go.'

It was over a month since she'd seen Alan Mill. Which was just as well, she told herself severely. Personal friendships were discouraged and though she had been involved in more than one investigation with the police officer, it was only right that their relationship should be confined to the occasional, fleeting professional contact. It was a definite weakness on her part to regret the excitement that sent the adrenalin coursing through her veins when they were engaged on a case which had dropped upon them out of the blue and which was missed when everything returned to normal again.

Their most recent collaboration had left her feeling vaguely disillusioned with the world,* more certain that her loyalties lay with the convent and her sisters there, so there was absolutely no excuse for the feeling of malaise that gripped her. It was probably the weather, she decided, genuflecting to the altar and climbing the spiral staircase.

'Is that you, Sister Joan?'

Little Sister David looked up from her desk just within the open door of the library. Sister David had the appearance of

* See *Vow of Fidelity*

someone destined by nature to be a librarian. Tiny and spare with thick spectacles and a skin that looked like the blank grey-whitened paper of a book, she had jutting teeth and a snub nose, and an unexpectedly pretty voice.

'I came up to contemplate some kind of strategy for clearing out the junk,' Sister Joan said. 'Am I disturbing you, Sister?'

'Not in the least.'

Sister David pushed up her spectacles and gave her sweet, timid smile.

'You're working on the children's book?' Sister Joan glanced at the tiny, neat handwriting that filled the page. Sister David only used the convent typewriter for her secretarial work.

'I'm up to J,' Sister David said. 'I've chosen St John the Beloved and St Joan of Arc to represent the letter. Their stories are interesting, don't you think?'

'Isn't being burnt alive strong meat for youngsters?'

'Actually the more horrid a story is the more children seem to enjoy it,' Sister David said with unexpected shrewdness.

'You're right, Sister. I'll leave you to it then.'

Sister Joan withdrew from the threshold of the library and went into the first of the huge storerooms which stretched over the rest of the chapel wing, joined by an archway, with large, grimy windows along the outer wall. The light here was dim even on a sunny day, the windows being not only smeared and dirty but partly blocked by the packing cases that were piled in tiers with narrow gangways between littered with bits and pieces of broken furniture and cardboard boxes bulging with old newspapers and piles of old books, their covers stained and torn. She had started to compile a local history of the district using old newspapers which needed to be sorted into chronological order, but the task went slowly partly because she could devote only a limited amount of time to it, partly because she had a bad habit of getting immersed in items that had nothing to do with the area at all. Nevertheless she was reluctant to throw them out.

There was a large wall cupboard, its door swinging on its hinges. It contained rolls of motheaten cloth and several stacks of documents. Once cleared it would provide an excellent receptacle for the old newspapers. Sister Joan pulled out a roll of musty brocade, its silk pitted with tiny holes, its raised embroidery greatly tarnished, and wrinkled up her nose.

Not even Sister Teresa could conjure dusters from anything like this. She would bring up some large sacks and fill them with what was outworn long ago.

Something slid from the mouldering folds and landed at her feet. Sister Joan bent and picked it up, moving nearer to the light. It was a photograph, sepia faded, the background a blur of obscurity against which the face appeared in stark relief, only blurred by a thick film of dust.

An arrogant face, she thought, her stomach churning as she stared at it. The dark eyes were heavy-lidded, the mouth full and sensual, the effect exaggerated by the narrow sideburns of black hair. She knew the face though she had met its owner only on a handful of occasions. Grant Tarquin stared at her mockingly. No, not him but his father or more likely grandfather surely. Intrigued she turned the photograph over and read the handwriting scrawled across the back, still black and bold after the years:

We have a secret the Devil and I.

That was all. Staring down at it, feeling the gloom of the storerooms close in about her, she was immeasurably relieved to hear Sister David call, 'Would you like to come down for a cup of tea, Sister?'

Two

She had pushed the photograph beneath the folds of decaying brocade again and left it there, scrubbing her hands in the little washroom with more than usual energy before following Sister David downstairs and over to the recreation room where the nuns, congregating from their various tasks, drank a cup of tea before going to the afternoon talk. This being Advent the subject of these talks was mainly centred upon the ideas of waiting and preparation. Sister Joan's mind wandered, something extra to put in her private spiritual diary, she thought, and wondered if after her death the journal would be circulated as an example of how not to be a nun!

'Sister Joan.'

Mother Dorothy was looking at her.

'Yes, Mother Dorothy?' Sister Joan jumped slightly.

'Forgive me for interrupting your meditation,' Mother Dorothy said, allowing no trace of sarcasm to enter her cool voice, 'but as Sister Teresa and Sister Marie will be going over to the postulancy after supper has been cleared away it would be a great help to us and save Sister Teresa from having to come back to the main house with these dark nights to add to her discomfort if you were to see to the final locking up when the grand silence begins, and also to give the morning salutation.'

'Yes, of course, Mother Dorothy. I shall be pleased to help out,' Sister Joan said. She spoke with absolute sincerity. Locking up, lowering the lights, checking on Alice and Lilith meant that she would have the place to herself for a little while after her sisters had retired to their cells. Late at night there was a peace that stole over the enclosure that was refreshing to the body and the spirit. Giving the morning salutation meant rising at 4.30 in order to wake the rest of the community at five, but it also meant half an hour in which to prepare oneself for the day ahead while the rest of the community still slept.

'Good. I take it that you will be starting the clearance of the storerooms soon?'

'Yes, Mother Prioress. Luther and Padraic have both offered help and Brother Cuthbert is ready to lift anything heavy.'

'Do try to do as much as possible yourself, Sister,' Mother Dorothy said. 'We don't want the house cluttered up with men.'

She spoke as if men were highly undesirable objects to be tidied away as fast as possible. Further along the semicircle old Sister Gabrielle emitted a barely concealed snort of amusement.

'*Dominus vobiscum*,' Mother Dorothy said. 'Yes, Sister, what is it?'

'I shall need large sacks, bin liners or something of that sort,' Sister Joan said.

'For the rubbish in the storerooms? Sister Martha, do you have any unwanted potato sacks?'

'I'm sorry, Mother. They were all used when we collected the fruit,' Sister Martha said.

'You will also need disinfectant, more scrubbing brushes and polishing cloths,' Mother Dorothy said. 'You had better take the van into town tomorrow morning and buy what you need. You may also buy a copy of *Exchange and Mart*. It would be wise to check on what prices are being asked for various things these days, so that if we do find any worth selling in the storerooms we won't offer them at a price that is inflated or ridiculously low. *Dominus vobiscum*.'

Her glance dared Sister Joan to interrupt again.

And now it was morning though the dark sky outside disputed the fact. There had been a time when Sister Joan had doubted if she would ever be able to wake up so early without outside aid. The old trick of asking a soul just released from purgatory to shake her pillow as they passed had never worked for her. All the souls released from purgatory in her vicinity simply flew up without even ruffling the hem of her pillow. Fortunately she had learned to wake herself at whatever hour was necessary and lay for only a few seconds before wakefulness cleared the mists of sleep from her brain and she pushed back the blankets and slid her feet into the cloth sandals that served as slippers while she washed her face and cleaned her teeth in the basin of cold water on the floor, reached shiveringly for her clothes, combed her short black curls into place and pinned the short white veil over her head. The ankle-length grey habit with its wide sleeves and a neat belt from which her rosary depended, the thick black stockings and laced black shoes were as familiar to her as her own skin, and leaving her cell with her eyes accustomed to the darkness she went along the gallery past the dining-room out of which the recreation-room opened, down the dimly lit curving staircase, across the hall to unbolt the connecting door to the chapel and then across to the passage which led past the infirmary and the dispensary into the big kitchen with its two tiny, now unoccupied cells. Alice greeted her with a sleepy wag of the tail.

Sister Joan put on the huge kettles to boil, measured coffee into the jugs, cut thick slices of the brown bread which, together with a piece of fruit, comprised the communal breakfast at 7.30, and went back into the hall to pick up the wooden clapper which was sounded to mark the start of the day.

A large piece of paper had been folded and thrust through the letterbox behind the front door. She went over to pull it in, feeling the usual mixture of annoyance and amusement. It was quite astonishing how often circulars were delivered by hand even here, and most of them hardly likely to appeal to nuns either! She recalled a series of pamphlets advertising a new beauty parlour that offered instant facelifts and colonic irrigation, and another from a matrimonial agency which Sister Gabrielle had to be dissuaded from sending a spoof reply to declaring herself to be an eighteen-year-old millionairess from Peru.

This particular circular was curiously apposite.

G.T. MONAM, SCRAP MERCHANT AND SILVERSMITH
If you have unwanted articles to be cleared please ring the number below. We give the highest prices. Delivery of refuse sacks, assistance with clearing and free estimates given on demand. Highest prices given.

There was a local number beneath. Sister Joan folded up the circular, thrust it into the deep pocket of her habit and took up the wooden rattle, mounting the stairs briskly, whirling it over her head as she raised her voice loudly.

'Christ is risen!'

'Thanks be to God,' came the voice from behind the prioress's door.

Sister Joan passed her own door, whirled the rattle and cried again, 'Christ is risen!'

'Thanks be to God!' Sister David sounded as if she'd been awake for ages.

In contrast Sister Perpetua sounded grumpy, Sister Katherine sleepy and Sister Martha as startled as if she were hearing the words for the first time.

Sister Joan returned to the kitchen, giving a final whirl of the rattle at the door of the infirmary where two voices immediately answered. The old ladies slept fitfully these days, she thought, and went into the kitchen to open the door for Alice.

By 5.30 they were in chapel, kneeling in their places engaged in private prayer until either Father Malone or Father Stephens came to offer a low mass at seven. Sister Teresa and Sister Marie slipped into their accustomed places, looking slightly out of breath while Sister Hilaria processed in, followed by the pink-smocked, white-bonneted Bernadette.

'Pink for postulants, navy-blue for novices and grey for the godly professed!' Jacob had mocked when she had tried to tell him something about the Order she was planning to join.

'And the prioresses wear purple,' she had said, wanting him to understand that she wasn't just running away but entering a disciplined and rational world. 'They are elected every five years and can't serve more than two consecutive terms. After they have been prioress they are entitled to wear a purple band on their sleeve for each term of office.'

'Stripes for Jesus!' Jacob had said, and she had known then the depth of his hurt because he never spoke against Catholicism just as she never argued with the Mosaic code which he affected to despise but which, in the end, had proved stronger than his love for her.

Ten years had gone by since then. Now she was thirty-eight

going on thirty-nine, with her desires disciplined and Jacob, with his lean semitic darkness and passionate temperament, was no longer part of her thinking. So why on earth had he entered her head now?

It was the photograph, she decided. Grant Tarquin had been dark and lean with piercing eyes and the same soft, deep voice that had characterized Jacob. There the likeness had ended. Jacob had been a good person, obstinate, intolerant, quick-tempered, but clean-hearted. Grant Tarquin of whom she had heard nothing since he had left the district had been corrupt, the nearest thing to evil she had ever brushed against. The old photograph must be of his grandfather whose son had sold the estate to the Order of the Daughters of Compassion shortly before his death. The sentence on the back with its chilling implications had been penned long ago, and had no relevance today.

Father Malone had entered and gone into the sacristy. There was a barely perceptible stir of pleasure among the community. Father Malone was as Irish as shamrock and his sermons were geared to the slowest intelligences in his congregation but he was always kind, always interested in having a chat over breakfast, always there when needed, while handsome Father Stephens, for all his erudition and charm, was more at home in the bishop's palace.

Sister Joan blessed herself and forced the photograph with its sinister sentence out of her head.

Later, standing with her cup of coffee in her hand, she listened to the conversation that eddied and flowed around her. Light, inconsequential chatter which provided a short period of relaxation before the day's tasks began – the cells to be swept, the floors to be polished and the meals prepared by Sister Teresa and Sister Marie, the morning mail to be opened and read by the prioress before it was passed to the sister for whom it was intended, Sister David busy in the chapel seeing to the flowers and candles, then hurrying to take dictation from Mother Dorothy before she ascended to the library to continue her own work, Sister Martha digging over the ground from which the vegetables had been plucked, Sister Katherine mending the linen, Sister Perpetua tending to the old ladies, Sister Hilaria instructing Bernadette in the minutiae of the rule over in the postulancy – and twenty minutes later she herself was free, driving the convent van through the open gates, her thick, grey winter cloak shielding her from the non-existent cold, money for her purchases in her pocket, and the convent receding as she guided the van along the bumpy track.

She had meant to ask Mother Dorothy if she ought to phone the number printed on the circular but Mother Dorothy would probably have instructed her to use her own judgement in the matter. Sister Joan considered it now and decided to wait. Time enough to start making phonecalls when she'd found anything worth any money. In any case Padraic had first refusal.

On her left the little schoolhouse with the old beat-up car outside in which Brother Cuthbert's flaming red head was usually buried when it wasn't bowed in prayer seemed deserted. It was the hour when he usually did his bit of shopping in the town, she reminded herself, and drove on, past the path that snaked towards the Romany camp and towards the town whose streets wound below the wilder aspects of the moor like neat ribbons on an uncombed head.

She parked in the car-park adjoining the railway station, and walked back to the main road. It was still early, shopkeepers winching back their shutters, sleepy eyed-assistants filling up the supermarket shelves, children on their way to school.

'Good morning, Sister Joan!'

As usual there was pleasure in Detective Sergeant Mill's voice as he crossed the road to greet her.

'Good morning, Detective Sergeant Mill.' She felt a corresponding pleasure.

'I thought we'd agreed it was going to be Alan, Sister.' He raised a thin, dark brow. 'The full title's too much of a mouthful unless it's an official occasion. Is it?'

'No, it isn't,' she said. 'I'm in town on a shopping trip but the supermarket isn't open yet.'

'In that case step into my office and have a coffee.'

'I ought not.'

'If you don't Constable Petrie may run you in for loitering,' he warned. 'He can't abide nuns cluttering up the streets.'

'I'd like to see him try!' Sister Joan grinned, then nodded. 'A quick cup of coffee would be nice. Thank you.'

They entered the police station where the desk sergeant

greeted them with a look of pleased questioning.

'No crime to solve this morning,' Detective Sergeant Mill said. 'Two coffees, please, if you will.'

His office was as neat and impersonal as a monastic cell. Seating herself, Sister Joan remembered that he was no monk, but a married man though his bleak surroundings gave no hint of domestic felicity elsewhere. She knew that he adored his two sons, and had given up the idea of divorcing his wife in order to try for a reconciliation, but that information had been volunteered and she never asked questions that impinged on his personal life.

'Nuns cluttering up the streets,' she echoed aloud. 'You sound like Mother Dorothy, though in her case she was referring to men cluttering up the storerooms.'

'Workmen in the enclosure?' he guessed.

'Not yet. We're clearing out the storerooms over the chapel wing, or rather I am since I'm the only member of the community at present without a definite job. Brother Cuthbert and Padraic and Luther all offered to help but Mother Dorothy wants the bulk of the work done before they're admitted.'

'Is there a lot of stuff up there?'

'A couple of hundred years' junk,' she said with a grimace. 'We're all hoping there may be something worth selling up there. Money's tight, as usual.'

'Money's tight everywhere. Why would the Tarquins have left anything valuable behind when they sold the property?'

'I doubt very much if they did, but the stuff needs clearing away. Oh, a circular arrived this morning coincidentally, advertising the services of a scrap-metal dealer and silversmith. Would you know anything about the firm? I know some of these people aren't always entirely scrupulous about their dealings.'

'You're scared of letting a Van Gogh go for a tenner?'

'I don't think I'd do that. Do you know G.T. Monam?'

She had taken the circular out of her pocket and passed it to him.

'Looks like a one-man operation,' Detective Sergeant Mill said. 'Very badly printed. I can find out the address for you if you like?'

The sergeant, coming in with the coffee, received his superior's brisk orders with a nod and went out again.

'So you're going treasure hunting?'

'Yes, though I don't expect to find anything. It's Mother Dorothy's way of making me feel useful.'

'Wouldn't you be more useful selling your own paintings?' he asked.

'Mother Dorothy thinks otherwise.' She kept her tone carefully neutral. 'After all I never got very far with my painting before I entered the Order. Now Sister David earns a fairly regular income from her translations, and the series of booklets on the saints she's working on for children will bring in more income once she finds a publisher.'

'Well, you know your own business best.' He gave a small shrug, looking up again as the sergeant came in.

'The number is that of an office on the industrial estate,' the latter said. 'I rang it and a young lady answered, offered to take a message for Mr Monam. I said it wasn't necessary and rang off.'

The industrial estate spilled over from the council estate on the far side of the moor. Sister Joan who'd never been there looked enquiring.

'Odds and sods of light industry – textile printing, a couple of warehouses,' Detective Sergeant Mill said, answering her unspoken query. 'Did you get the address, Cummings?'

'Number thirty-four, in the Nightingale complex, sir. I wrote it down.'

'I might call round and get a free estimate,' Sister Joan decided, pocketing the slip of paper on which the address had been written. 'The supermarket will be open now so I'd better go and get my purchases. Thank you for the coffee.'

'Any help you need with the clearing out, Sister, you know where to come.' The detective sergeant had risen.

'That's very kind of you.' Her eyes sparkled with amusement. 'I've had so many offers of help that if I accept them all we'll be falling over one another up in the store.'

'Do you want us to make any further enquiries about this Monam fellow?' he asked.

She shook her head. 'No, I probably won't bother. Padraic and Luther can help out and they'll probably charge less.'

'Better than getting cheated by cowboys,' the sergeant said. His tone suggested that nuns were more liable to be cheated than most. It was childish of her but the remark rankled.

In the supermarket she bought the largest bin liners she could find, a couple of stiff scrubbing brushes, cloths, several bars of strong soap, a couple of large bottles of disinfectant and, as an afterthought, a flask of insect repellent. She piled the lot into the van, strapped herself into the driving seat and, without making any conscious decision, turned the vehicle, not towards the track that wound up on to the moor, but down the main street which curved round to join the council estate with the newer industrial estate stretching its tentacles beyond. Now that she was actually in town it would do no harm to check out the estimate. The sergeant's obvious belief that she was an innocent likely to be cheated had irritated her. Mother Dorothy was of the opinion she had worldly leanings; Sergeant Cummings who was new to the station had looked at her as if she spent all her days wrapped in astral clouds and never came down to earth at all.

She turned off into the council estate, feeling as she always felt on the rare occasion she was obliged to go there slightly depressed. The houses were neat, the small gardens carefully tended, the roads straight, with a cluster of small shops every few yards, but they all looked the same. Neatly printed notices informed her that a neighbourhood watch scheme was in operation, and the few people she saw looked happy enough, but she wondered how often any of them left the comfort of their little houses to wander on the moors where a semblance of ancient wildness could still uplift the heart.

A sign directed her to the industrial estate and her spirits sank lower as she drove over an underground walkway into streets lined with buildings that were still raw and new with the remnants of building materials in the plots of earth and gravel that were still to be turned into gardens. At the end of each street a high block of offices obstructed the view, windows blank glass, overflowing bins standing forlornly waiting for collection. Already scraps of newspaper and rusting tins were scattered in the gutters and the whole place had a defeated air. The high blocks had been named after famous women, a sop to feminism in a place where women's rights, she guessed, were not much observed. There were a couple of betting shops, a covered arcade of shops, a bingo hall and a youth centre with garish posters advertising some rap group plastered all over the walls. A group of youths sprawling on the steps stared after her as she drove past, only mild curiosity in their faces. At the next corner the name Nightingale Court was printed in black on a huge noticeboard.

She turned in at a wide gap in the high, surrounding walls and found herself in a large car-park with several vehicles already parked. On all sides concrete rose, pierced by row upon row of large windows with the kind of glass that repels anyone who hopes to glance inside. One or two of the upper windows were open and she glimpsed a brave pot of chrysanthemums making a splash of colour, but apart from that the prevailing shades were grey, black and a dingy white.

'Brave new world,' she found herself muttering as she parked close to one of the entrances and got out to push open the heavy swing door.

Within was a bare wall with a list of firms slotted into the wall and two lifts. Several of the wall slots were occupied by 'For Rent' announcements. Obviously there was still a good deal of unused office space here. She stepped nearer, ascertained that number thirty-four was on the third floor and to be reached by taking Lift 1, and stepped inside, feeling the customary discomfort in the pit of her stomach as she pressed the button and the doors silently closed.

NUN STARVES TO DEATH IN BROKEN LIFT.

It was a disconcerting headline to flash into her mind. Ridiculous too! Clearly many of the offices were already rented out and the lifts constantly used, but there was an atmosphere of – no, there was no atmosphere at all, she corrected herself. This was a shell which stripped its occupants of humanity. It reminded her of the high-rise apartments into which slum dwellers had been moved during her own schooldays. Clean, hygienic, easy to maintain and completely lacking in soul, so that the new occupants had missed the easy camaraderie of the grimy alleys and small houses of the past and become neurotic and depressed with the community spirit vampirized out of them by grey and black and dingy white.

She stepped out thankfully into a corridor which bent at right angles to left and right. There were numbers on the walls with arrows pointing out the direction to them. Sister Joan located number thirty-four and walked to the right.

There were doors, some of them half-glazed, down both sides of the passage. Cards slotted into brackets at the side of each door showed which offices were being used and which remained to be rented. Thirty-four had no card by it and she frowned as she tapped on the door.

'Come in!' The voice was young and female, sounding startled. Sister Joan opened the door and went in.

The office was about twelve feet square, containing a flat-topped desk with a manual typewriter on it and two hard-backed chairs from one of which a young woman in her twenties with fair, curly hair had just risen.

'You're not G.T. Monam,' Sister Joan said pleasantly.

'No, I'm Mr Monam's secretary, Jane Sinclair.' The girl had a faint London accent and wore a white blouse and dark skirt.

'Sister Joan from the Order of the Daughters of Compassion. Our convent is on the moors.'

'I'm afraid I don't keep any money on the premises,' Jane Sinclair said apologetically. 'I've some change in my purse so if you don't mind—'

'I'm not collecting for anything,' Sister Joan broke in. 'In our Order we're expected to earn our own living as far as possible. Mr Monam isn't in?'

'I'm afraid not. Please, won't you sit down, Sister?' The young woman sat down herself, looking unaccountably relieved. 'May I help you?'

'I came for an estimate.'

'An estimate?' Jane Sinclair looked at her blankly.

'About the circular.' She took the folded paper out of her pocket and laid it on the desk. 'This was put through the door this morning. It so happens that we are about to clear the convent storerooms, so naturally I thought it a good idea to make some enquiries.'

'Oh, the circular. Yes, of course.'

'It does say that free estimates are provided,' Sister Joan said patiently.

'Estimates.' Jane Sinclair repeated the word as if it were couched in an unfamiliar foreign language. Then her brow cleared. 'Yes, of course. It'll be in the files.'

She rose again, crossed to a filing cabinet, and took out a slim folder.

'Yes, here it is.' She took out the single sheet of paper it contained and looked at it. 'I'm so sorry, Sister. Mr Monam did mention an estimate for clearance. It's based on the hours to be worked. Seven pounds an hour. I don't know how much you'll have to—?'

'I don't know myself yet,' Sister Joan said. 'Seven pounds an hour. Thank you. If it's necessary I'll be in touch.'

'There's a note to say the price can be lowered through mutual agreement.'

'I see.' Sister Joan hesitated, then said, 'When does Mr Monam come in? I might be able to negotiate with him personally.'

'Oh, he doesn't come in at all,' Jane Sinclair said. 'At least he hasn't since I joined the firm.'

'But surely—?'

'Oh, this isn't Mr Monam's office,' the other said. 'I actually work for the Falcon Typing and Telephone Answering Service, taking messages for people, typing the odd invoice, that sort of thing. Mr Monam must be a client of theirs.'

'But surely – you've met him?'

'I've spoken to him on the telephone. Late yesterday afternoon. He rang up and said that if anyone came in and asked for an estimate I was to give it to them.'

'He didn't give you the estimate?'

Jane Sinclair shook her head.

'There are various files in the cabinet,' she said. 'I've only worked here a couple of days so I'm still finding my way round. To tell you the truth I don't think I'll stick the job for very long. It's a bit lonely being stuck here all day in an unlocked office.'

'Surely you can lock the door?'

'There's no money kept here, only the telephone and the typewriter is an old one,' Jane Sinclair said. 'I was a bit nervous when you knocked at the door. You're the first person who's come since I started.'

'How did you get the job in the first place?'

'I've been temping – you know, doing temporary secretarial work. Then the manager of the Falcon Company rang my agency, saying someone was needed in the Nightingale office, so I came along here.'

'And met the manager?'

'Mr Shrimpling, yes. He told me what I had to do and then left.

The company's a fairly new one and the last secretary left to get married and they wanted someone in a hurry. It's quite legitimate; the agency always checks these things.'

'I'm sure it is.'

'Office rents are so high these days that lots of small firms use these kind of places to do business, take messages and so on,' Jane Sinclair was continuing.

'And you have a list of the clients?'

'That's confidential, but yes I do have a list. Mr Monam's name is on it.'

'I see.' Sister Joan bit her lip, obscurely uneasy without knowing why.

'His is the last name on the list,' Jane Sinclair said, opening up a little. 'He became a client yesterday as a matter of fact. He registered with the Falcon Company and asked me to take messages.'

'So his name wasn't on the original list that Mr Shrimpling gave you?'

'I rang him up to check that G.T. Monam was registered and Mr Shrimpling said to add his name to the client list myself. Someone rang earlier to ask.'

'A friend of mine,' Sister Joan said, beginning to rise. 'You wouldn't have had anything to do with the printing of the circular, I suppose?'

'Sorry.' The other took another glance at it. 'It looks a bit smeary and amateurish,' she said.

'Yes it does. Well, thank you for your time anyway.'

'It was a nice change to have someone to talk to,' Jane Sinclair confessed. 'You know most of these offices are empty and there's no security in the building. Just about anybody could stroll in.'

'One last thing!' Sister Joan wondered why she hadn't thought of it before. 'If Mr Monam only registered as a client with the Falcon Company yesterday afternoon how did the estimate come to be in the files? Someone must have called round with it.'

'Nobody came – at least not while I was here,' Jane Sinclair said. 'I left at five-thirty and went home.'

'Leaving the door unlocked?'

'It can be locked from the outside, but the key's a bit stiff when you try it on the inside. Yes, I locked the door, but it wouldn't be hard for someone to break in. But why should they?'

'Do you have an address or phone number for Mr Monam?'

'No. I suppose Mr Shrimpling might have one. I can give you the address of the main Falcon office if you like.'

'That's very kind of you.'

Writing it down neatly, Jane Sinclair said, 'It is a bit funny when you come to think of it, isn't it?'

'Funny' wasn't the word that Sister Joan would have used.

Three

There had been no time to pursue her enquiries. Feeling slightly guilty at the steps she had already taken she drove back through the industrial estate and turned off on to a side road that would bring her eventually out on the moor. The estimate was too high anyway. It was better to get Padraic and Luther to cart away anything they might be able to find a use for, and forget the badly printed circular, but the small discrepancies nagged at her. Apart from anything else it seemed decidedly odd that within hours of her being told to clear out the storerooms someone had registered with the Falcon Service and managed to get a circular pushed through the front door of the convent and a copy of the estimated charges into the files of a locked office. However, since it was none of her business, she had no reason to make any further enquiries.

Having lugged her purchases out of the van, she hurried up to lunch. As always she was struck when she entered the huge room leading off the upper landing by the contrast between what it had once been and now had become. Once large banquets had been served here on long tables resplendent with white embroidered cloths and delicate china and crystal glasses. The guests – it was said that King Edward VII when Prince of Wales had been a visitor here – had talked and drunk their toasts and toyed with the food on their plates before the ladies, at a signal from the hostess, had risen and retired into the drawing-room through the double connecting doors to drink coffee while the gentlemen settled to their port and brandy. Now only the polished floor and the silk panels on the walls remained. One long table with benches and stools ranged along both sides and a chair for the prioress at the head, a wheeled table on which the simple courses were set out, and a lectern with the book being currently read aloud on it comprised the whole of the furnishings. Bowls of soup, sandwiches of tomatoes and beansprouts and a large dish of pink fleshed pears had replaced the myriad courses previously enjoyed. Everything had the beauty of absolute simplicity. Only the choice of book jarred slightly. Sister Hilaria whose week it was to read had chosen the story of St Lawrence who had been grilled alive. It was an unhappy coincidence that Sister Teresa had provided toasted sandwiches.

Lunch over, the nuns dispersed to continue their tasks until the daily discussion at four o'clock. Sister Joan left the table and went down the stairs and up into the storerooms again. From her place in the library Sister David waved an abstracted hand.

The roll of motheaten brocade still held the sepia-tinted photograph she had found the previous day. Sister Joan drew it out and stared at it again, the same shiver rippling through her. The Tarquins had been an ancient family, tracing their line back to the fourteenth century, tempering their political and religious convictions to the prevailing wind. In such a long line there must have been villains and saints, but it was disconcerting to come across a tangible reminder of one, assuming the sentence on the back of the portrait referred to the front. She pushed the picture back and walked on along the narrow aisles between the piles of boxes and broken furniture.

It would be a good idea to clear out the larger pieces first and establish a working space for herself. She disentangled a couple of cobwebbed kitchen chairs and carried them on to the landing. Both chairs were broken and neither of them had ever been designed by Chippendale or Sheraton. They'd do very well for firewood in the kitchen and the infirmary, the only parts of the convent that were heated. They were also light enough to take down the spiral stairs.

By four she had carted a decent amount of potential firewood into the stable. A couple of sagging sofas and a Victorian conversation seat with torn fringing would have to be winched down from the windows or broken up into smaller pieces. It was a great pity that a wall blocked access from library and storeroom to the upper floor of the rest of the house.

'I see that you've been busy, Sister.'

Mother Dorothy lifted her brows as Sister Joan came into the parlour.

'Yes, Mother Prioress.'

Too late she realized she hadn't bothered to don an apron and her habit was covered with specks of dust.

'You will want to confess a fault against cleanliness at general penance,' Mother Dorothy said, 'but for now you're excused from our discussion while you tidy yourself.'

'Thank you, Mother Dorothy.' Sister Joan genuflected, started to wipe her hands on her skirt, spotted her superior's face and thought better of it.

She hurried to the kitchen, rolled up her sleeves and scrubbed the grime off her hands and forearms. A clothes' brush removed most of the dust and bits of fluff from her habit, and she rubbed her shoes with an old piece of towelling. As she came out of the kitchen again the telephone rang.

'Cornwall House. Sister Joan speaking.'

Usually it was the laysister who answered the telephone but the rules about it were fairly relaxed.

'Oh, you're the sister who came in this morning!' a voice said. 'Jane Sinclair?'

'From Nightingale Court, yes.' The other sounded rushed and nervous. 'Could you meet me, Sister? I've found out something rather peculiar but I don't want to talk about it over the telephone.'

'I can't walk in and out of the convent whenever I feel like it,' Sister Joan said. 'I have to get permission from the prioress.'

'I could meet you tomorrow morning at the café in the High Street,' Jane Sinclair said. 'The one with the hanging baskets outside – do you know it?'

'Yes, I do. Can't you give me some idea?'

'I'd rather not. You might think I'm being silly anyway. Ten o'clock tomorrow morning? It's my day for going in late. Do try and get permission, please.'

'Yes, of course, but I wish you'd tell me—'

'It's about the cemetery,' Jane Sinclair said.

'The cemetery?'

'The resurrection – the Tarquin family graves – oh, I can't explain over the phone. I'll see you tomorrow, Sister.' The receiver was replaced before Sister Joan could answer.

She hung up frowningly and retraced her steps to the parlour thoughtfully. Jane Sinclair had sounded frightened and bewildered. What that had to do with the cemetery and resurrection she couldn't begin to imagine. Perhaps the secretary was merely one of those people who thought nuns were romantic and who tried to scrape acquaintance with them by any means possible, but she had seemed to be just an ordinary, not very quickwitted young woman.

Fortunately the need to ask permission for another trip into town was removed the next morning when Sister Teresa asked her after breakfast if she would collect some groceries from town.

'I ought to have asked you to get them yesterday,' Sister Teresa said, 'but Sister Gabrielle wasn't too well during the night and I came over from the postulancy just in case I was required but thank God, I wasn't. Only it sent the groceries clean out of my head, and I do hate driving the van. I barely scraped through my driving test and I haven't done any at all since I came into the Order.'

'Provided Mother Dorothy agrees I'd be glad to go into town,' Sister Joan said promptly.

'That's awfully kind of you.' Sister Teresa's round young face was filled with the most guileless gratitude. 'Yes, Mother Dorothy said I could ask you. She wasn't very pleased at my forgetfulness. It isn't as if we can afford to use unlimited amounts of petrol.'

She sighed as she spoke as if the lecture she'd received had overcast her spirits, but a moment later she was humming under her breath as she scrubbed the step. Sister Teresa wasn't a person who held on to misery or made a great parade of her conscience.

Sister Joan drove into town with a remarkably clear conscience. The errand had obviously been engineered by Providence, saving her from having to explain anything to Mother Dorothy who almost certainly would have refused leave to waste any petrol on a wild goose chase.

As she passed the track branching off towards the Romany camp Padraic hailed her from the saddle of a suspiciously new-looking mountain bike.

'Good morning, Sister! You started clearing out the rubbish

yet?' He pedalled up to the van as she braked.

'I've made a start but it'll be weeks before everything's done. Padraic, did you mention to anyone that we were clearing out the storerooms?'

'I didn't but Luther's been gabbing about it,' Padraic said. 'Very proud that he's going to be helping out when the time comes. It wasn't a secret, was it?'

'No, of course not. I just wondered because we got a circular through the door advertising a scrap merchant and silversmith.'

'Both of them at once?' Padraic's lean brown face displayed surprise.

'Apparently. A Mr Monam. Do you know of him?'

'Monam? No, never heard of him.' Padraic was clearly running a list of names through his head. 'No, that's a new one on me. Some Johnny-come-lately, if you ask me. I'll get you the best prices and I won't do you down. You know that, Sister.'

'Indeed I do,' Sister Joan said. 'Though I doubt if there's anything worth selling up there. Where did you get the bicycle?'

'This?' Padraic looked down at the gleaming machine as if he hadn't noticed it before.

'That,' Sister Joan said firmly.

'I found it. I *found* it.' He shot her a beatific smile.

'And now you're on your way to the police station to hand it in. That's very public spirited of you,' she approved. 'Constable Petrie will be delighted.'

'You're a hard woman, Sister Joan.' He admitted defeat with a grin and a wink. 'Yes, I'm handing in lost property. Public spirited!'

'Good!' Sister Joan drove on, stifling a chuckle. Padraic Lee was a lovely man but articles that fell off lorries were liable to stick to his fingers.

She bought the groceries that Sister Teresa had listed, stowed them in the back of the van, and walked back to the High Street. Strictly speaking she should have asked for permission to drink a coffee in town but Mother Dorothy had always made it plain that the sisters were expected to use their own judgement. At this particular moment Sister Joan's judgement informed her that she'd better find out what Jane Sinclair had to say to her.

The café was almost empty at this comparatively early hour. She sat down in a chair at a window table and ordered a black coffee. It was just gone ten so the secretary would be there at any moment.

She had sipped her coffee slowly and twenty minutes had gone by. Obviously Jane Sinclair had thought better of keeping the appointment, unless she'd been summoned early to work, in which case she'd very likely ring the convent again and try to fix another appointment for which permission was hardly likely to be given.

Sister Joan paid for the coffee, went back to the van and turned it in the direction of the industrial estate.

It was a windless day, the air still and warm and clammy. Torn posters on the billboards that lined the streets hung limp and dead, painted slogans peeling, and the few people around moved sluggishly as if the energy were being sucked out of them.

She parked in Nightingale Court and ascended in the lift, following the arrows along the upper corridor to the office she had visited the previous day. The door was closed and the card with G.T. Monam wasn't in the bracket at the side. She knocked briskly and waited. Nothing. Stepping back she raised her voice,

'Miss Sinclair, are you there? It's Sister Joan!'

No answer.

She tried the handle but the door was locked. Jane Sinclair had mentioned it could be locked from outside. Clearly she wasn't there. Held up somewhere? In any case there was no more time to be spent on looking for her. Sister Joan took out her small notepad and biro, scribbled her name on it, adding, 'Sorry I missed you', slid it under the door, and turned away. If Jane Sinclair decided to contact her again then she'd have to insist on being given the information over the telephone. Going down in the lift again she suppressed a feeling of annoyance. People who didn't keep appointments were not her favourite people.

The van was unmolested. Despite the generally run-down appearance of the district its citizens must be fairly law-abiding. She climbed in and started the engine. The engine coughed, spluttered and died. Peering at the petrol gauge, she was dismayed to find it on Empty. She'd filled up recently and there ought to have been plenty left.

'Sister! Sister!'

Someone was tapping on the side window. A brash young face with spiky yellow hair and a safety pin tastefully slotted through an earlobe grinned at her.

'Yes?' She wound down the window a few inches.

'Your petrol's been siphoned off,' the teenager said.

'I rather guessed that,' Sister Joan said ruefully. 'Did you see who did it?'

'Wouldn't say if I had,' the youngster said. 'Name's Jem. Jem Cuttle.'

'Sister Joan.'

'There's a garage not far off. Someone'd come out with a can of petrol,' Jem Cuttle said. 'I could watch the van for you in case the wheels get nicked.'

'For a consideration I suppose?' She was already climbing down.

'A pound?' The lad looked hopeful.

'Fifty pence,' Sister Joan said, fishing for a coin. 'You've got a nice little racket going here, haven't you? Next time pick on someone with more money. Nuns never have any.'

'Turn second left then first right. The garage's there,' Jem Cuttle said, grabbing the fifty pence. 'You want me to look after the keys?'

'No, thank you very much.' She clutched them firmly as she turned away.

It took several minutes to locate the garage and buy a can of petrol. Money was being wasted at an alarming rate, she thought, trailing back to Nightingale Court where, not greatly to her surprise, she found the van abandoned and no trace of the youthful entrepreneur. By the time she had replenished the tank, driven round to the garage to return the can, and got herself back on to the main road again the morning was well advanced. At the café she parked briefly and went in without much hope to see if Jane Sinclair was waiting for her. The tables were occupied by customers, mainly housewives taking a break from their shopping, but there was no sign of the fair-haired young secretary.

Coming out she ran full tilt into Constable Petrie who was scowling at the van as ferociously as his pleasant young face could manage.

'You're on a double yellow line, Sister,' he informed her. 'By rights I ought to be giving you a ticket.'

'Oh, don't let the habit stop you,' she said bitterly. 'A fine for illegal parking will just round the morning off nicely.'

'I was going to say – by rights I ought to give you a ticket for illegal parking if I didn't know you were engaged on a mission of mercy,' he said with dignity, and went off trying to look as if he hadn't seen her at all.

This was not, she thought resignedly, climbing up into the driving seat, going to be her day! That thought made her drive back over the rough moorland track with more care than usual though her heart sank again as she saw Mother Dorothy advancing purposefully towards her.

'You've been a very long time, Sister,' she said sharply as Sister Joan alighted from the vehicle.

'I'm sorry, Mother Prioress. I had a cup of coffee while I was in town.'

'And lingered over it!'

'And then I was further delayed because someone siphoned out the petrol. I'll pay for it out of my own pocket money.'

Two pounds a week was supposed to cover all personal necessities like stamps and writing paper and the unscented skin cream that was the only sort allowed.

'I shall expect you to pay half,' Mother Dorothy said, not troubling to waste her breath on recriminations. 'Did you report it to the police?'

'It wouldn't have done any good, Mother. There wouldn't have been any way of catching them.'

'Crime is becoming rife even in our corner of the world,' Mother Dorothy said. 'You had better take the groceries into Sister Teresa.'

Mercifully she hadn't enquired when the petrol had been stolen. Obviously she had presumed that it had happened in the town car-park while Sister Joan was drinking her coffee. It was less complicated to leave it like that, Sister Joan decided, and jumped slightly as her superior said, 'There was a telephone call while you were out.'

'For me?'

'No, Sister. Why would you imagine any call was automatically for you? It does concern you indirectly however.

A gentleman rang to enquire if we had any valuables to sell. It's astonishing how some people imagine we dwell in the midst of medieval splendours! I told him that to the best of my knowledge we hadn't and he thanked me and rang off. It occurred to me afterwards that perhaps I should have mentioned that you were engaged in clearing out the storerooms but you did mention that Padraic Lee would be helping clear out the larger pieces.'

'Yes.' Sister Joan hesitated, then asked, 'Did the gentleman give his name?'

'He was a Mr – Trent, I believe. His voice wasn't very distinct though it may have been a bad line. A dealer in antiques, I assumed, though why he rang us up I can't think. Sister, the groceries!'

'Yes, Mother.'

Sister Joan dived hastily into the back of the van and lugged out the large cardboard box.

There was no further opportunity that day to ponder over the information she had been given. Not until the community had settled for the night and she lay on the narrow bunk in her cell could she allow recent events to unroll in her mind. First the decision to clear out the storerooms, then after she had spoken about it to Luther and Padraic the amateurishly printed circular thrust through the letterbox, her own visit to the office in Nightingale Court and her meeting with Jane Sinclair, the telephone call from Miss Sinclair and her failure to keep the appointment made and now, in her absence, the telephone call to Mother Dorothy from a man calling himself Trent. Someone, she thought, turning over on to her side in flat contradiction of the rule that nuns should compose themselves for sleep on their backs with folded hands lest they died in their sleep, was exceedingly interested in the contents of the storerooms. The sooner she got down to the work the better! She turned over on to her other side, and fell asleep, her last conscious thought being that if she did die during her sleep God would simply have to take her as he found her.

After breakfast the next morning she slipped down to the telephone and rang the office in Nightingale Court, but the telephone went on ringing without answer. She replaced the receiver, scowled at it, then lifted it again and dialled the police station.

'Constable Petrie?'

'Yes, Sister.' He had recognized her voice at once. 'I'm manning the desk this morning. Nothing wrong, I hope?'

'First, thank you for letting me off with a caution yesterday,' she remembered to say. 'I wondered if you could tell me anything about a firm that hires out typists and secretaries on a temporary basis – the Falcon Typing and – I can't recall the rest.'

'The Falcon Typing and Telephoning Answer Service,' Constable Petrie supplied. 'Yes, it's quite a big company, got branches all over the south-west. Very good reputation. My cousin worked for them for a time.'

'Do you have their telephone number?'

'Hold on a minute!' She heard the rustling of the pages of the directory and then the number, repeated slowly in Constable Petrie's warm Cornish tones.

'Thank you, Constable. Thank you very much.'

Ringing off she redialled and was greeted by a blare of music and a voice requesting her to hold on.

'Falcon Typing and Telephone Answering Services. May I help you?' The voice was brisk and female.

Sister Joan hesitated, guessing that the agency was unlikely to divulge details of its employees over the telephone.

'My name is Sister Joan,' she said cautiously. 'I'm ringing from Cornwall House.'

'Is that a hospital?' the woman at the other end of the line enquired.

'No, it's a convent. The Order of the Daughters of Compassion. I'm ringing about an – an acquaintance of mine. A Jane Sinclair. I was supposed to meet her for coffee yesterday morning but she didn't turn up and she wasn't in her office either. It's rather urgent that I contact her so I wonder if you had her home address?'

'We're not actually supposed to give out such information,' the woman's voice said, 'but as you're a nun – Miss Sinclair has a flat in Cemetery Road. Number twenty-two.'

'Thank you, that's very helpful.'

'Miss Sinclair's a very nice girl.' The voice had warmed. 'She's received some excellent recommendations from previous employers for whom she worked.'

'Thank you.'

Sister Joan hung up as Sister Perpetua came down the stairs, her reddish brows shooting up.

'You've got a busy social life, Sister,' she commented.

'It was business,' Sister Joan said uncomfortably.

'Well, I hope the business brings in sufficient to meet the telephone bill at the end of the quarter,' Sister Perpetua said. 'You spent a lot on cleaning materials too. Insect repellent for heaven's sake!'

Sister Joan bit back the retort that Sister Perpetua was the infirmarian and not the treasurer and said meekly, 'I was afraid that I might bring a few fleas into the main house, Sister.'

'Well, get along then.' Sister Perpetua's usual good humour had returned. 'And put an apron on this morning. Sister Katherine has quite enough to do without having to scrub your habit every other day!'

'Yes, Sister.'

There was no opportunity to make any further enquiries. Sister Joan went into the kitchen and donned her apron, collected some bin liners, bestowed a pat on Alice and sent a smile to Sister Teresa who was washing up.

'At least someone looks cheerful this morning,' she remarked.

'Have you had a run in with Sister Perpetua?' Sister Teresa lowered her voice. 'She slept badly last night she told me. She kept dreaming that someone was walking round and round the building.'

'She isn't usually so snappy, though,' Sister Joan admitted. 'I must try the patience of a saint sometimes. Don't bother to confess anything this evening because my sins will take up the whole hour.'

'You sound quite proud of that,' Sister Teresa said with a grin.

'One more sin to add. Have a nice day, Sister!'

Entering the chapel she met Sister Perpetua again, the older nun having just risen from her knees.

'Sister, do forgive me for being so abrupt just now.' Sister Perpetua had flushed unbecomingly. 'It was quite inexcusable of me, but I seem to be snapping everybody's head off this morning.'

'Perhaps you slept badly?'

'As a matter of fact I did, though that's no excuse for ill-temper,' Sister Perpetua said. 'I was dreaming on and off that someone was creeping round the building. I kept half-waking and deciding that I'd better get up and investigate but then I fell asleep again and found myself in the same dream. Anyway I shall put it out of my mind now. Do you need any help up in the storerooms?'

'I promise to call on you if I do,' Sister Joan said tactfully, blenching slightly at the thought of Sister Perpetua's large feet and enthusiastic cleaning methods let loose among objects that were old and delicate.

A few minutes later she was on her knees burrowing into a pile of mouldering rags that were fit only for the dustbin. The stink of them was stomach churning. She thrust the last of them into the bin liner and stepped to the window to tug it open and let in some air and more light.

Further illumined, the narrow aisles between the piled boxes revealed a thick patina of dust in which her own footprints could clearly be seen. Sister Joan stared at them, stared at the line of smaller prints that ran alongside. Round prints like those made by an animal save these were not pawmarks. They ran up and down between the boxes in an almost straight line, turning and coming back again as if some creature with tiny feet had paced the storerooms up and down, up and down.

'Sister Joan?'

Sister David's voice from the doorway made her start violently and swing around.

'I'm sorry. I didn't mean to startle you, Sister!' Sister David looked like an apologetic rabbit. 'I wondered if you needed any help before I began on the library lists. Oh, how odd!'

She too was staring at the prints.

'It looks as if a large cat got in here,' Sister Joan said casually.

'Or someone walking on tiptoe. How peculiar!'

'Not wanting to be heard, I daresay. Maybe one of the children from the village sneaked in.'

'Well, the outside door into the chapel corridor is never locked,' Sister David said. 'You know, Sister, I sometimes think that's a mistake. Not to leave the chapel unlocked because it's a lovely idea knowing that anyone can come in to pray or just sit quietly at any time, but there are some quite old books in the library and even though I keep some of the more valuable in a locked cupboard I do worry about them.'

'We could get a bolt fixed on the outside of the library door.'

'Would that cost very much?' Sister David asked worriedly.

'Oh, I'll treat you,' Sister Joan said as airily as if her pocket money were not already mortgaged to the extra petrol she'd bought.

'That's very kind of you.' Sister David looked pleased. 'What about the prints? Oughtn't we to tell someone?'

'Nothing seems to have been disturbed,' Sister Joan said, looking round, 'so I don't see any point in worrying the others. I'll get a bolt fixed on the library door for you. Are any of the books very valuable?'

'Oh, I hope not!' Sister David clutched the book she was holding as nervously as if it were a long-lost child. 'If there are then I shall feel obliged to suggest that we offer them for sale, our finances being in such a shaky condition.'

'Cheer up. We might find something worth some money among this lot,' Sister Joan said cheerfully.

'Oh, I would think the Tarquins removed anything like that when they sold the estate,' Sister David said practically. 'It was old Mr Tarquin sold it, wasn't it?'

'Yes, just before he died. He moved to a big house on the outskirts of town. That was before I came here.'

'We none of us ever met him. Father Malone said once that he gave away nearly all his money to charity. Well, I'd better get on.'

'Without mentioning the cat,' Sister Joan reminded her.

'Whatever it was it can't have been a cat,' Sister David said, peering through her thick spectacles. 'Not unless you have cats as big as large dogs! Anyway it looks like the print of the front of the undersole of a shoe.'

'Some kid walking on tiptoe and poking around.'

'Or a devil worshipper.'

'A – what?' Sister Joan's head jerked up.

'Devil worshippers always walk on their toes when they're in consecrated places,' Sister David said. 'Didn't you know that, Sister?'

Four

By lunchtime she had tied several piles of old newspapers into bundles and put them in the wardrobe where the rolls of motheaten cloth had been packed. She had also conquered her initial impulse to destroy the old photograph and put it in a large envelope on top of the newspapers. The prints she had mopped out but faint traces of their outlines still remained as if the storerooms had been touched by something impossible to eradicate.

Sister David hadn't elaborated on her remark but had returned to the library. Sister Joan had debated with herself whether or not to show her the photograph but decided against it. There could be no connection between a man whose photograph had been taken at least seventy-five years before to judge by the cravat he wore and the sepia tones of the print and a fresh set of half-footmarks. Sister David, in any case, was nervous in temperament, and spent several hours a day closeted alone in this part of the house.

So far she had found nothing of any possible importance. A dozen bags of rubbish waited to be carried downstairs and she began lugging them after a hasty glance at the little steel fobwatch pinned to her habit. With so much weighing against her being late for lunch was something she couldn't afford.

'I'll give you a hand with those, Sister!'

Sister David trotted from the library and seized two of the bags.

'Thank you, Sister. That's very kind of you.' Sister Joan was already halfway down the spiral.

From above Sister David said, panting slightly as she heaved up one of the bags, 'I've been thinking about the prints. I'm sure they must have been made by some youngster who sneaked up here when nobody was looking. I'm only surprised it hasn't happened before.'

'Not a devil worshipper then?' Sister Joan reached the bottom of the stairs and set down her load.

'I don't know what on earth made me say such a foolish thing.' Sister David had flushed. 'It was something I read once when I was doing research on something quite different and it just popped out of my mouth. Mother Dorothy is so right when she warns us that the tongue is a dangerous weapon. I hope you won't allow the remark to worry you.'

'I'm not the worrying kind,' Sister Joan said cheerfully. 'Hand me down the next two, Sister, if you will. There's nothing here that would be the least use on Sister Martha's compost heap so we'll sling them at the front gate ready for the council lorry. And we'd better wash our hands or Mother Dorothy will imagine that we've taken up coalmining!'

They genuflected to the altar and went along the corridor together.

'Sister Joan, I think you ought to give Lilith a gallop,' Mother Dorothy said, as the simple meal drew to its close. 'The ground is still somewhat soggy but there must be a side road you can exercise her on.'

'There's the old road that leads past the municipal cemetery,' Sister Perpetua said. 'Not much traffic there if I remember rightly. Mind you it's years since I was out that way so they might have built a motorway there by now.'

'I'm sure Sister Joan will notice it if they have,' Sister Gabrielle said.

'Give her a good long ride,' Mother Dorothy said. 'This mild weather can't last for long and then she'll be shut up in her stall for most of the time.'

'Yes, Mother Dorothy.'

God worked in mysterious ways, Sister Joan reflected, as she pulled on the blue jeans she was permitted to wear beneath her habit when she went riding. Outside a weak sun sent pale rays down to the moist dark earth.

'If you ride off to the left just before you get to the council estate,' Sister Teresa said, following her into the yard, 'you'll come to Cemetery Road in about five minutes. There are some old houses on the right that've been turned into flats.'

Sister Joan waved her hand, gathered up the reins and rode out beneath the archway. Lilith had been a fixture when the Daughters of Compassion had bought the estate and must be over twenty by now and past middle age in equine terms. She served no useful purpose since the van was used for shopping and since the little school had closed down there was no need for Sister Joan who had taught there to use her as transport. She supposed that the pony was an unjustified expense but it would be heartless to get rid of her at this stage in her life.

She rode at an easy pace over the moor, enjoying the fresh air and the sweeps of browning grass with the occasional pools of emerald where the rain had fallen most abundantly. Here and there a patch of purple showed where the heather had mistaken the season and continued to bloom. Pausing on the crest of a rise she saw the roofs and trim gardens of the council estate spread below with the taller tenements of the industrial estate beyond. It was Saturday and Jane Sinclair was unlikely to be in her office but she might be at home.

The track broke away at the left to curl around the base of a hill. Sister Joan branched off on to it, allowing herself a small lift of anticipation. This was a road she hadn't had occasion to follow before and she felt a further glow at the knowledge that she was obeying Mother Dorothy's instructions and not rushing off impulsively.

At the bottom of the long slope the road turned to left and right, with rows of headstones on the left and a row of elderly looking houses on the right. They had been handsome dwellings once but were run down now, lacking paint and unbroken tiles, the iron gates sunk into the weedy gravel of the drives. She resisted the temptation to dismount outside number twenty-two, and turned instead to the left, riding through a gateless gap into the cemetery itself.

It was the perfect example of a burial ground used for hundreds of years and now too full to hold any more bodies. The headstones were crammed together, ranging in style from the classical columns of eighteenth-century white stone through to the massive and convoluted memorials of Victorian England with one section of plain stone crosses where those who had fallen in the two great wars were buried. Here and there she spotted the wax flowers under glass domes that had always struck her as ugly, but most of the graves were weed-covered with the ubiquitous bramble spearing and hooking the high grass. At the far end guarded by yews was a stone building with a nail-studded oak door.

Probably the old chapel of rest, she decided, dismounting and tethering Lilith to a ring in the wall near a stone trough filled with rainwater. There was plenty of grass here for the pony to nibble while she herself walked up to the door and gave it an experimental push. The heavy door wheezed slightly as it swung open slowly and she stepped inside, the interior gloom relieved by the shaft of light through the opened door.

It had been a chapel once, was probably still consecrated even if it was no longer used. At the eastern end flanked by granite columns was a stone altar with a cracked and filthy stained-glass window high in the wall behind it. There was a stone plinth topped with wood that had probably served as a lectern and several benches piled up higgledy-piggledy against one wall. There were few things sadder than a place of worship where nobody worshipped any longer. Sister Joan walked up the aisle and turned in to a space at the side of the altar which looked as if it had been added on as an afterthought.

There were several stone tablets in the walls here and scarcely perceptible names carved on them in memoriam, two narrow tombs with reclining stone figures atop them, a brass of a knight with a helmet stuck jauntily on the side of his head. There was also dust, thicker here in this neglected corner than elsewhere. Sister Joan looked down at the double line of half footprints that circled the tombs and shivered with more than the cold.

Whoever had tiptoed through the storerooms had tiptoed here too. She stepped closer to look at the tombs, the hairs at the back of her neck crinkling as she transcribed the Latin inscription.

Sir Richard Tarquine, servant of the Lord, born in the Year of Grace, 1400, knighted by Milord Warwick and departed this life in the Year of Grace 1466.

The figure on the tomb had been carved from life she

guessed, looking at the flaring nostrils, the eyes set beneath winged brows above high cheekbones, the wide, full-lipped mouth. Sir Richard had died in his bed to judge by the sheathed sword in his hand, the supine relaxation of the legs. Sir Richard Tarquine whose descendant Grant Tarquin was as like him as it was possible to be.

She was conscious of the silence, of the little spirals of dust arising under her own sensible shoes, of a waiting quality in the disused air. Devil worshippers walked on tiptoe. That was what Sister David had said. Jane Sinclair had spoken of the cemetery and of resurrection.

'I'd better see if she's at home,' Sister Joan said aloud, and resisted the urge to whistle defiantly as she left the sad, neglected little chapel.

Lilith, raising her head from her snack of sweet grass, gave her a look of deep reproach.

'Sorry, girl.' Sister Joan loosed the reins and led her along the path. An elderly man had just come through the gap in the wall and gave her a disapproving look.

'The Council doesn't like the hunt coming through here,' he said.

'I'm not hunting,' Sister Joan said, wondering if that was quite true. 'Well, not foxes anyway. I haven't damaged anything.'

'You're a nun, aren't you?' He blinked at her shortsightedly.

'Yes. I'm Sister Joan from Cornwall House – up on the moor.'

'The old Tarquin place?' A gleam of interest came into his face.

'Did you know the family?' she asked eagerly.

'Know them?' he echoed. 'I worked for them, didn't I? Years ago when I was a lad. Just after the war it was. Sir Robert was there then, of course. A real gentleman he was! Always had a smile and a civil word for me. Very well liked in the district he was – and his lady wife. She wasn't a well woman, not a well woman at all. It was a real surprise when young Grant was born. Sir Robert was that pleased that he bought champagne for everybody on the estate. He might as well have saved his money seeing young Grant turned out so wild.'

'They didn't get on?' she prompted.

'Sir Robert now was a real nice person,' the elderly man said, clearly launched on a tide of sentimental reminiscence. 'Always had a kind word. Young Grant acted like he owned the county – oh, very charming and polite if there was a lady in the case but for ever screwing money out of his dad and then spending it – horses, the dogs, drink – you name it! It was a big shock to him when the old man died – not that he was old, only in his fifties but the way his son acted had aged him before his time. And then he was lonely after his wife's death too.'

'You were saying it was a shock when he died.' Sister Joan brought him back to the main point.

'Young Grant expected to inherit everything,' the other said. 'He was the last of the family after all, but there wasn't much left. He'd had most of it before his dad died, but there was still the big house and the land. Oh yes, he expected to get that!'

'He left instructions for it to be sold cheaply,' Sister Joan said.

'That's right, Miss – Sister!' The other slapped his thigh suddenly and chortled. 'And him not even a Catholic! Sold it cheap too so there wasn't much for young Grant to get his hands on! I reckon it was justice done.'

'And then Grant Tarquin died? I heard he had died.'

'About a year ago – eighteen months. Died broke too.' He chortled again. 'Spent everything and his own house went to pay off his debts. So that was the end of the Tarquins. Seems a pity somehow, a grand old family coming to nothing. His was the last funeral in this cemetery as a matter of fact.'

'Where?' Sister Joan asked.

'Over in the corner there. There are Tarquins all over the graveyard. There's talk of putting a preservation order on the old chapel, but I don't know if they will. If you ask me there are things more worth preserving.'

'Did you work for Grant Tarquin at all?' Sister Joan enquired.

'No, I left in – let me see – 1969. I used to look after the cars and do odd jobs but then I was offered a good job with a proper pension here in town – Mundy's Garage and Vehicle Repair Service. I was wed by then and I fancied a bit of independence. Sir Robert was all for it, told me that I ought to better myself, and gave me a very handsome leaving present – enough to put down a mortgage on a little house. But it was sad in a way to leave the old place. My dad and grandad worked there before me. I recall my dad telling me some tales of old Sir Grant

Tarquin, that was Sir Robert's father after whom young Grant was named. And my dad's dad had worked for Sir Grant's father – Devil Tarquin.'

'What?'

Sister Joan who had been feeling slightly confused as she tried to get relationships straight in her head jerked up her chin, her usual response to a shock.

'On account of he worshipped the Devil,' the other said, lowering his voice slightly.

'Surely not!'

'So the tale went. According to what my grandad told my dad who told me about it. Sir Richard Tarquin who was Sir Robert's grandad was a real rake – wine, women, song, if you'll excuse the expression, Sister. Oh, there were some wild doings up at Tarquin House in those days. Even talk of murder though I think my grandad must've misremembered that. It's true though that he never went to church. His son got his own back though. He buried him in consecrated ground anyway.'

'Here?'

'In the chapel, Miss – Sister. Right next to the Sir Richard who fought in France during the Hundred Years' War. We did that war in school.'

'Yes, so did we,' Sister Joan said. 'I did see two tombs in the chapel, but I didn't look closely at the other one.'

'It looks old, doesn't it?' He chortled again. 'It's a fake though. Real stone and all that but carved in 1903 when Devil Tarquin died. His son was a Godfearing religious man and he was set on leaving his dad in holy ground.'

'I daresay he wasn't as bad as rumour had it,' Sister Joan said.

'My grandad told my dad he was worse,' the other said. 'Handsome though! Young Grant took after him – black eyes and hair and loads of charm. Charm isn't a good thing to have, Sister. Makes a man careless of doing the right thing. That's what my wife says anyway. "Don't you go trying to charm me, Daniel Cobb", she says, "for it never came natural to you, thank the Lord!"'

'Well, I've found your company very pleasant, Mr Cobb,' Sister Joan said, laughing despite herself. 'You must have lots of interesting memories. Unfortunately I'd better be getting back.'

'It was a real pleasure meeting you, Sister!' He held out a

gnarled hand and shook hers vigorously. 'It's a treat to chat with a nice young lady, and there's no danger of my Minnie going on about it because you being a holy nun makes it all right, doesn't it?'

'Like Caesar's wife,' Sister Joan said solemnly, 'we're above suspicion.'

He grinned to show he appreciated the quip and trudged past her. There were still so many good, decent people in the world, she reminded herself. Ordinary people who had not been brainwashed into believing that evil was something imagined in the mind.

Leaving Lilith tethered again she hurried back along the path to the little chapel. She wanted to take a quick look at the second tomb though even to herself she couldn't have given any logical reason.

Pushing open the door and entering the gloomy interior took an unexpected effort of will. Nothing had changed. The halfprints were still circling the tomb of Sir Richard Tarquine. She stepped to the other tomb with its recumbent knight, marvelling at how authentically medieval it looked. The inscription on the side was, however, in English.

Here lie the remains of Sir Richard Tarquin, Born 1840.
Died 1903. Rest in peace.

And of course he was resting in peace, she told herself. His nickname of Devil Tarquin must have been exaggerated. Mustn't it?

The light was imperceptibly fading, her shadow growing taller and thinner as she left the chapel and retraced her steps, curving away from Lilith in order to reach the part of the cemetery where Daniel Cobb had pointed out the burial site of Grant Tarquin.

The plain marble headstone had clearly just been set and the long mound at its foot was covered with couch grass that strangled the wild flowers springing from the soil. In stark lettering the bare essentials were provided for the casual visitor.

Grant Tarquin
1945 – 1994

The knightly prefix had been omitted and there were no words of pious comfort. He had been a comparatively young man, she thought, and from what she knew of him a man eaten up with rage and driven by his own twisted desires. She must remember to pray for his soul.

Walking on a little further she found more Tarquins, their details faint now, their headstones mossy, half-sunken in the ground. Beyond them a column surrounded by rusted railings bore lists of Tarquins and their wives, many buried with small children. The Tarquin men seemed to have rotated the names of Richard, Robert and Grant, she noticed, peering through the railings, and feeling a twitch of amusement as she spotted a John. Obviously a misfit!

The outlines of the headstones were blurring into a still, moist twilight. She was going to be late and she hadn't yet called at number twenty-two to find out if Jane Sinclair was at home. Straightening up she turned and went back to where Lilith was tethered. Had been tethered! With a sensation of annoyance mingled with alarm she stood looking at the dangling rein. How the – how on earth had the ageing pony tugged free? She was the most placid of animals and if she had escaped she'd certainly had help. Sister Joan picked up the end of the dangling rein and looked at the neatly cut edge of the leather.

Someone had sneaked up to cut through the rein and lead Lilith silently along the broad grass verge into the road. But who would do such a thing? Horse thieves were hardly likely to seek their profits in a cemetery!

It really was growing misty, white trails of vapour wreathing the crooked headstones and drifting over the long grasses. There was no sound here save the occasional far off hum of a car. She shivered, aware of – no, not of being alone with the dead. That wouldn't have troubled her one whit. Graveyards were generally peaceful places that held no horrors for her. But something here was different. She had the distinct impression that someone – something? – watched her from somewhere just out of sight. There was nothing to be seen even when she swung round, but her hands, thrust deep into her pockets, were clenched fists, her jaw set.

'Is anyone there?' She raised her voice. 'Who are you?'

There was no answer. What on earth had made her think that there might be? She was alone with the rising mist as it thickened and curled into shapes that clung to the edges of the headstones, dense as ectoplasm.

'Lilith! Lilith! Here, Lilith!' She raised her voice again but nothing answered. Only the mist shapes grew and hung silently in the air.

A footstep cracked the gravel by the gap in the wall. She opened her mouth to call again and found herself mute. Another footstep. Someone moving towards her through the mist. Suddenly and shamingly her nerve faltered and she turned, fleeing along the path towards the memorial column where she crouched, gripping the rusted railings, trying to control her breathing.

Behind her something moved, slid like a dark shadow just outside her line of vision. She sensed rather than saw it and sprang up, calling out again in a rediscovered voice that shook with strain.

'Who are you? What do you want?'

The footsteps on the gravel quickened and broke into a run. A torch shone in her eyes, and she flung up her arm to shield them.

'Taken up grave-robbing, have we, Sister?' Detective Sergeant Mill enquired genially.

'Alan!' She used his Christian name spontaneously. 'Alan, someone cut Lilith free and then – there was someone here, behind me for an instant. A few seconds ago.'

'There's nobody around now.' He shone his torch around.

'Oh, how can you possibly tell?' she exclaimed, irritated. 'The mist's getting so thick and there are so many headstones, so many monuments – what are you doing here anyway?'

'We found Lilith a few minutes ago,' he said, not answering the question. 'Trotting up the road towards the moor. Constable Petrie is taking her back for you.'

'And you heard me calling?'

'I heard someone calling. This damned mist distorts sounds and shapes. It's not like you to be scared of shadows.'

'I'm not,' she said with dignity, 'only of the things that make the shadows.'

'You should watch fewer horror movies,' he advised.

'We're not allowed to watch any movies as you well know.'

'So you get your entertainment from headstones.'

'The place is full of Tarquins. I knew they were an ancient family but I hadn't realized how far back they went, how many died young.'

'Well, they're all gone now,' he said in a practical tone. 'Come on, Sister. I'll run you back to the convent. I'd like a few words with you anyway.'

'About what?'

They had reached the road where the police car was reassuringly parked.

'Let's sit inside. It's getting chilly.'

Lowering herself into the passenger seat she waited while he positioned himself behind the wheel.

'I have to ask you a few questions.' He frowned, tapping the wheel with his knuckles.

'You sound very official.'

'Sorry! It's a bad habit. I merely wanted to clear up something, that's all. Is this yours?'

He had taken a slip of paper out of his pocket, switching on the interior light so she could read it.

'Yes, I wrote it.' She handed it back. 'I went to see Jane Sinclair but she wasn't in her office so I scribbled this and pushed it under the door.'

'You say in it that you're sorry you missed her. Did you have an appointment?'

'She rang up and asked me to meet her for coffee yesterday morning. I waited in the café but she didn't turn up so I went to her office to see if she was there. It was locked so I wrote the note and put it under the door.'

'How did you come to know Jane Sinclair?' he asked.

'I had a circular pushed through the letterbox advertising the services of a Mr Monam who buys scrap metal and stuff. We're clearing out the two storerooms so – but you know this already. Constable Petrie checked on the telephone number for me. I went there.'

'And?'

'It's just a branch office for a firm that relays messages and things. Jane Sinclair hadn't been there for very long.'

'Fair-haired, about twenty-two or three.'

'Yes. Not very bright, I'm afraid, but very pleasant. She had an estimate of charges from Mr Monam.'

'He'd given it to her?'

'No. It was in the filing cabinet. She was a bit puzzled about that because he was a new client who'd registered with the agency over the telephone so she couldn't work out how his estimate sheet had got into the files. She was a bit nervous in the office. There's no way of locking the door properly from the inside and there's no proper security in the building.'

'A child could pick the outside lock. I'm surprised you didn't try.'

'No, of course I didn't! I thought the estimate was a bit high – Padraic and Luther will help cart away the rubbish without charging very much. And then she phoned the convent and asked me to meet her for coffee.'

'Without saying why?'

'She said she was worried and she mentioned the Tarquins and resurrection,' Sister Joan said slowly. 'She wouldn't say any more until we met but she did sound worried – oh, and she mentioned the cemetery. She has a flat in Cemetery Road and as I was giving Lilith some exercise I thought it wouldn't hurt to find out if she was at home.'

'Did you go to number twenty-two?'

'I turned aside into the cemetery so Lilith could crop the grass a bit.'

'And you went tomb spotting.'

'Something like that. Alan, how did you know it was number twenty-two where Jane Sinclair lives? And the note? How did you get my note?'

'The office where she worked was broken into early this morning. Someone coming into one of the other offices saw the damage and phoned the police.'

'And you found the note. I see. No, I don't! Why were you called to a simple break-in?'

'I wasn't. Constable Petrie went round at lunchtime just after we got the call. He found your note and he found Jane Sinclair.'

His voice had not altered. It remained calmly official but she stiffened in her seat, her blue eyes darkening as she looked at him.

'Something's happened to Jane Sinclair, hasn't it?' she said.

'Constable Petrie found her. She'd been strangled,' he said.

Five

'Poor girl.' Her hand rose to bless herself as she murmured, 'May her soul and the souls of all the faithful departed rest in peace.'

'Religion has a sentence to fit every occasion, doesn't it?' he said bitterly.

'It doesn't imply lack of feeling.' Her blue eyes were dark with pain. 'When one has no adequate words for something terrible the approved formula does help sometimes though I realize that's hard for you to understand.'

'Sorry, Sister! What I just said was completely out of order. Look, I was on my way to her flat to find out what I could when we spotted Lilith. Constable Petrie's ridden her back and I can drive you back at once but—'

'You prefer to see the flat first. Yes, so would I.'

'I'll get Petrie on his mobile and assure him that you're safe and he's to wait at the convent until I pick him up.'

'That will set Mother Dorothy's mind at ease,' Sister Joan said, hoping that it would.

She waited while he made the brief call, forcing herself to calmness. What had happened was shocking and sad but there was no way of bringing Jane Sinclair back to life and getting in a panic would help nobody.

'We'll drive to the flat. It's only a couple of minutes down the road,' Detective Sergeant Mill said, starting the engine.

The large house was a remnant of the Georgian age. The woman who opened the front door looked ordinary, anxious and a trifle flustered.

'Police? Have you any news of Miss Sinclair?' she demanded. 'I'm getting really worried about her. She's not the kind of girl to stay out two nights in a row. I've never known her do such a thing before!'

'You're the owner of the house?' Detective Sergeant Mill enquired.

'I'm Anne Dalton, yes. I keep the ground floor for myself and rent out the second and third floors. They've been converted into flats, very nice and not very expensive. My main concern has been to have nice, quiet people in. Miss Sinclair came here about six weeks ago and old Mrs Trevelyan has been here for five years.'

'This is Sister Joan from Cornwall House,' he broke into the flood. 'I'm Detective Sergeant Mill. I'm afraid the news isn't good.'

'You'd better come in.'

Belatedly she held the door wider, ushering them into a square hallway with stairs opposite. 'Please, in here. Do excuse the mess. I wasn't expecting – what's happened to Miss Sinclair?'

'A body has been found in the office where she worked. We believe that it's hers.'

'In Nightingale Court? Oh, that's a very nasty, cold building! She said she felt nervous working there. All those layabouts hanging round! Please sit down!'

She was hastily gathering up knitting and magazines that were scattered over couch and fireside chair.

'I'd like to see her flat first. There was a key in her handbag which I assume – perhaps you'd like to sit down for a moment yourself?'

'I think I will,' Anne Dalton said, sitting down abruptly. 'I'll be quite all right in a moment, honestly. It was just – not that it was exactly a shock. I've had such a funny feeling ever since – she never stays – *stayed* out all night. Always so polite and pleasant. Yes, do go up. She's on the top floor. I'm afraid there's no lift.'

'Perhaps you'd like to make some tea?' Sister Joan suggested.

'Yes of course!' The woman was on her feet again, clearly glad to have been given something to do. 'You go on up and I'll put the kettle on. Yes, tea is very good for shock, isn't it?'

She bustled into the back as they mounted the stairs.

'Did you want me to help with the tea?' Sister Joan asked.

'No, I need you as a witness to forestall any bright lawyer who might pop up in the future and say the police planted or removed something.'

'I thought lawyers served justice.'

'They serve their clients and earn their fees,' he said wryly, fitting the key into a door at the top of the second flight of stairs.

They stepped into a narrow hall which was clearly part of the original landing. To the left and right were doors; opposite was a round window. Sister Joan went to it and looked down across a narrow alley into the cemetery, now blotted out by mist.

'Not a very cheerful view,' Detective Sergeant Mill remarked, glancing over her shoulder.

'You can see the little chapel from here,' Sister Joan said thoughtfully.

'So let's find out what's to be seen indoors!' He opened the door on the left and went into a large sitting-room with an obviously adapted kitchen leading off it.

The room was undistinguished, its white paintwork faintly yellowed, its carpet an indeterminate swirl of browns and greys, the furniture fairly modern and the wallpaper faded. There was a small television set in one corner, some paperback romances in a bookcase, two flower prints on the wall. On the coffee table were a few women's magazines and a plastic bag containing a half-finished knitted sweater in pale blue.

In the kitchen everything was neat and in place, the cups and saucers ranged on a shelf, some ready meals and a cheesecake quarrelling with a diet sheet sellotaped to the fridge door.

'What do you think?' Detective Sergeant Mill glanced at her.

'She hadn't been here long enough to impress her personality on the place,' Sister Joan said.

'What was it like – her personality?'

'I only met her the once on the day I went to the office. She was very pleasant, a bit naive, inclined to be nervous because she was on her own in the office, quite glad to talk even to a strange nun. Just a nice ordinary girl.'

'And that nice ordinary girl arranged to meet you for coffee because she had something important to tell you and never turned up.'

'She said it was her morning for going in late to the office so we agreed to meet at ten. She must've called in at the office earlier before coming to meet me – I wonder why.'

'And found someone there already? Someone who'd broken in?'

'Isn't it unusual for a burglar to strangle someone?' Sister Joan asked. 'I'd have thought he'd be more likely to hit her over the head before making his getaway.'

'You're right, Sister.' He frowned consideringly, then walked into the hall again and opened the right-hand door.

Sister Joan followed reluctantly as he switched on the light and moved to draw the curtains across the misted windows. To enter someone's bedroom with the object of looking through their belongings went against all her instincts. Only the knowledge that somewhere here might lie a pointer to her killer made it bearable.

The bedroom with its adjoining bathroom was decorated and furnished with the same lack of style as the rest of the flat. There was a paperback romance and a box of sweets on the bedside table, jeans and sweaters and T-shirts in the shelves down the side of the wardrobe in which hung a summer jacket, a pinafore dress and two summer dresses with ribbon shoulder straps and bolero jackets. The colours were mainly pink and blue and the shoes at the bottom of the wardrobe neatly ranged and polished.

'Very conventional,' Detective Sergeant Mill said.

'Not in every respect.'

Sister Joan had opened a drawer to reveal a tangle of scarlet underwear, lacy and almost transparent. Beneath the scraps of net and lace was folded a black nylon nightgown, its bodice transparent, ruffles round the hem.

'She had a boyfriend then?' He stared at them.

'I don't think so,' Sister Joan said. 'I think these were part of her dream life.'

'What makes you say that?'

'She struck me as a lonely girl, not having friends. The books she read were all very mild romances and she seems to have liked knitting and watching television. I think she bought these for herself. They made her feel glamorous and desirable. I might be wrong, of course.'

'She was a virgin anyway. The police surgeon checked on that.'

'So it wasn't a sexual murder?'

'Apparently not.'

'Poor Jane Sinclair!' Sister Joan closed the drawer and swung round, her cheeks reddening. 'This makes me so angry! A nice, ordinary girl – a decent girl with dreams of passion and romance and cheated of any hope of it, cheated of the rest of her life by – who?'

'Better ask why,' he advised.

'I don't know.' She scowled at her reflection in a mirror hanging on the wall.

'There was nothing in her handbag but her chequebook, her keys, some tissues, and an address book with only a few addresses pencilled in. We've contacted her parents by the way. They're coming down tomorrow to make a formal identification and arrange the funeral. Sister, think hard! What could she have wanted to see you about?'

'I think it must have been about Mr Monam,' Sister Joan said slowly.

'I thought she mentioned the Tarquin family.'

'Grant Tarquin. She said something about resurrection. Grant Tarquin's buried in the cemetery over there.'

'You're not suggesting he's come back to life, are you?'

'No, of course not! As far as I know she'd never even heard of him.'

'And how does that tie in with the mysterious Mr Monam?'

'I don't know.' Sister Joan moved to the window and lifted the curtain, gazing out into the mist, collecting her thoughts. 'That was the name on the circular that was pushed through the convent door and a Monam had registered with the telephone answering service, by phone. Did you find out anything about that?'

'I rang the main office this afternoon. It's a bona fide organization. The clients pay a set fee to have messages relayed and passed on to them. Mr Monam paid by cash, sent notes through the mail which is unusual. And we don't know when his estimate sheet was put in the files.'

'How was Jane Sinclair supposed to send on messages to him?'

'She wasn't. He said he'd phone in himself once or twice a week. Another point. You seem to have been the only one favoured with a circular. Petrie made some extensive enquiries but nobody else has had one of those circulars.'

'Then he must have wanted to get into the convent storerooms,' Sister Joan said.

'Who knew you were clearing them out?'

'Well, we've talked of doing it for ages but I did tell Luther who was asking if there was any work for him and Padraic told me that Luther had been chattering about it all over the place. Someone in the pub or in town might have heard him, I suppose, but it doesn't make sense. If someone wanted to cash in on any scrap metal or old silver we found, all they had to do was come to the convent and present the estimate. Why all this elaborate secrecy?'

'Mr Monam does seem slightly elusive,' he said. 'Anyway we're checking up on all the clients of the answering service. What does the late Grant Tarquin have to do with any of this?'

'Nothing,' Sister Joan said. 'Grant Tarquin's dead.'

'Not resurrected?' He cocked an eyebrow at her.

'Of course not!' she said sharply.

'But you're holding something back.' It was a statement, not a question.

'When I find out something that's relevant I'll tell you,' she said.

'Don't wait too long, Sister.'

His dark eyes held her blue ones for a moment. She nodded slowly.

From downstairs Anne Dalton called quaveringly, 'Shall I bring the tea up?'

'We're just coming down.' Detective Sergeant Mill ushered Sister Joan ahead of him, locked the door leading into the flat and came down the stairs.

'I kept it hot.' There was a faint reproach in her voice as they entered her sitting-room.

'This is a sad inconvenience for you, I'm afraid.' He sat down on one of the upright chairs and favoured her with one of his most charming smiles. It was a smile intended to dispel alarm and put a possible witness at ease. Sister Joan observed it with a feeling of affectionate amusement.

'It's sad altogether, isn't it?' Anne Dalton passed the teacups. 'Help yourselves to sugar. Oh, and the biscuits are homemade.

Miss Sinclair was quite partial to my biscuits. She did her own bit of cooking, of course, but once or twice we had a nice cup of tea together. It was the first time she'd been away from home, you know. Oh, her parents—'

'They've been informed. They'll be coming on Monday.'

'Here? I'm not sure whether—'

'They'll be staying over at an hotel,' he reassured. 'However they'll want to see her flat, I daresay, and pack up her things. The forensic chaps will want to have a look first though. Have you another key to her flat?'

'Yes, but I've never used it,' she said. 'I'm not the kind of landlady who pokes and pries.'

'Obviously not but for the moment we'll be needing it ourselves.'

'It's here.' Looking slightly offended, she reached up and took down a key from a hook on the wall. 'Was there anything else?'

'Did she have any visitors while she was living here?' he asked.

'No, nobody at all.' Anne Dalton sipped her tea with a ladylike air. 'Not that I'd have objected, mind! I made it clear that she was welcome to invite friends. I wouldn't have said anything if one had stayed overnight. One has to be broadminded these days, if you'll excuse my saying so, Sister. But she didn't know anyone in the district, spent most evenings up in her flat, watching the television and knitting. She showed me the pattern.'

'She didn't go out at all?'

'She went to the cinema in town once and she sometimes went for a walk. At dusk, after she'd had her tea. She said it was nice to be able to take a quiet stroll and feel safe, but I told her not to be too confident. There are some nasty types live over on the council estate.'

'Did she walk in the cemetery?' Sister Joan asked abruptly.

'I'm sure I don't know.' The landlady looked surprised at the question. 'It's not everybody's idea of a cheerful stroll, is it? Not that it isn't peaceful and some of the old gravestones are quite interesting – you wouldn't believe how many women died in childbirth a hundred years ago, but all the same—'

'Well, we won't be troubling you any further.' Detective Sergeant Mill set down his cup.

'You don't think it might be a maniac about?' The elderly

woman looked at him with eyes anxious in her crumpled face. 'I always make sure to lock up properly and see the windows are all right and tight.'

'I doubt it but it's always wise to take sensible precautions,' he approved. 'Oh, I take it she didn't drive a car?'

'She could drive but she didn't have one of her own,' Anne Dalton said. 'She walked to work.'

'And she kept regular hours there? At work, I mean?'

'Set off at eight-thirty every morning except Friday, and she didn't work at the weekends. Except yesterday.'

'Yesterday was different?'

'She left at eight-thirty as usual. Seemed a bit excited but she didn't say why.'

'It wouldn't have taken her an hour and a half to walk to the café,' Sister Joan said. 'She must've decided to call in at the office first.'

'She didn't say she was going early to work?' He glanced at the landlady.

'No. She just went off. Perhaps the gentleman who phoned up had some message for her.'

'What gentleman?'

He had spoken a touch too sharply. Anne Dalton's face set obstinately.

'I don't pry into my lodgers' private affairs,' she said. 'A gentleman telephoned and asked to speak to Miss Sinclair at about eight o'clock that's all I know. There's a telephone in the hall and I called up to let her know she had a call, that's all.'

'And she came down to answer it. You didn't happen to hear—?'

'I heard her say "Jane Sinclair here" and then I went through to the back to put some scraps on the bird table,' Anne Dalton said frostily. 'When I returned indoors she was just coming down the stairs with her jacket on. She said something like, "I'll see you later, Mrs Dalton" and went out. I assumed she'd gone off to the office as usual but your asking made me recall it was Friday.'

'Did the caller give his name?'

'No. I should have asked for it – I always do if anyone rings up but it was still early and I wasn't thinking.'

'Did Jane Sinclair get many telephone calls?' Sister Joan asked.

Anne Dalton shook her head, tucking a stray strand behind her ear.

'Her mother rang a couple of times and an old schoolfriend rang her up. She told me that she and her friend were hoping to get together when the friend came down to Cornwall in the summer.'

'Did she mention the friend's name?' Detective Sergeant Mill asked.

'Susie something or other. They hadn't met for years.'

'That seems to be all then. A couple of the police team will be along later to make more detailed checks on her rooms. We'd like to get that finished with before her parents come.' He rose, absentmindedly helping himself to another biscuit.

'Would you like one, Sister?' Anne Dalton proffered the plate. 'You've not eaten anything.'

'I'd love one but I'm in enough trouble already up at the convent,' Sister Joan said lightly. 'I seem to be running in circles to catch my own tail these days.'

'They must be very strict at the convent,' the other said sympathetically. 'Like being back in Victorian times I shouldn't wonder!'

'Well, we're spared whalebone corsets,' Sister Joan said.

'They do look uncomfortable, don't they?' Anne Dalton agreed. 'Interesting to look through those old photographs though, don't you think? All sitting up so straight with feathers in their hats! I've had many a smile over some of them.'

'You collect old photographs?'

'My late husband did. He liked old things. Always going off to auctions and such like. He brought back several old photograph albums during his time. Sometimes when I'm feeling a bit low I get them out and have a look through them. I was only showing them to Miss Sinclair a few nights ago. She came down for a cup of tea with me and I had one of the old albums out so she was looking through it.'

'I don't suppose that I could borrow it, could I? The one she was looking through?'

'Yes, of course you can, Sister. It's in the bookcase.' Anne Dalton crossed to it and drew it out. 'This will be particularly

interesting for you. The album came from the Tarquin house –
you call it Cornwall House now, don't you? Keep it as long as
you like.'

'Thank you,' Sister Joan said. 'That's very kind of you.'

'Seems funny that we sat here looking at those old photographs,' Anne Dalton said, 'and not knowing what was going to
happen in the next couple of days to the poor girl. Life's very
odd, isn't it?'

'Very.' Sister Joan took the album firmly and risked another
question, conscious of the detective hovering in the hall near the
front door. 'You were looking at this recently, you say?'

'Thursday – no, Wednesday evening. Quite late on actually.
Usually I try to be in bed by eleven but there'd been a good film
on television and I wasn't too sleepy so I popped upstairs to see
if Miss Sinclair fancied a pot of tea and a bit of a chat.'

'And she was up?'

'Staring through the landing window into the old graveyard,'
Anne Dalton said. 'Mind you, she told me she liked looking out
there. Some people wouldn't, you know. She came down for the
tea and we chatted a bit and I showed her the album. She took it
upstairs, as a matter of fact, to have a look at it and brought it
down the next morning.'

'Did she seem – was there anything in her manner that struck
you as different?' It was a risky question to ask since many
people were apt to imagine things after the event. Anne Dalton,
however, didn't seem to be one of these. She answered at once,

'Not that I noticed, Sister. She was a bit pale but we'd sat up
late chatting.'

'Thank you for the loan of the album,' Sister Joan said, tucking
it under her arm. 'I'll see you get it back very soon. And thank
you for the tea.'

'I think I might make myself a fresh pot,' the landlady said. 'All
this has upset me more than I care to let on. You never know
what's coming next, do you?'

'Indeed you don't.' Sister Joan smiled and hurried out to
where Detective Sergeant Mill waited.

'Sorry I was so long,' she apologized as they got back into the
car. 'I wanted to smooth over the rough edges. You were a bit
abrupt with her, you know.'

'You're right.' He threw her a rueful look as they drove off. 'I'm afraid it's a case of kicking the dog because you've had a bad day at work.'

'Murder cases don't usually have that effect on you.'

'They don't exactly fill me with joy either,' he said. 'Oh, it's not only that. Home life isn't all roses!'

'I'm sorry,' she said in a tone that warned him not to say any more, not to transgress the bounds they had set.

'I intend going to the pub and having a stiff whisky,' he said. 'Feel like joining me, Sister?'

'And get excommunicated? Don't tempt me!'

Equilibrium restored they grinned at each other.

'I'll have to make do with Constable Petrie then,' he said. 'All that chat at the end – I assume it had a point?'

'It might help fill out the picture,' she answered. 'Jane Sinclair rang me on Thursday and asked me to meet her the following morning.'

'Mentioning Grant Tarquin and the cemetery.'

'And resurrection. Obviously she didnt want to go into details over the phone. It occurred to me that the chat with Anne Dalton the previous night had something to do with it – maybe something that was said or something she saw. The album comes from the estate.'

'I heard. It sounds like a long shot.'

'Do you want the album yourself?'

'You look at it, Sister.' He sounded tolerant. 'If there's anything worth anything in it then let me know. I have to concern myself with the nitty gritty of the enquiry. Fingerprints, measurements, possible leads, you know.'

He sounded weary. Now wasn't the moment to tell him about the footprints in the storerooms and the little graveyard chapel. She said meekly, 'Yes, of course.'

They had turned on to the moorland track. Around them the mist crept whitely, pressing against the windows, stroking long, damp fingers down the glass. Even inside the car the air felt clammy. The lights of the convent were dimly glowing patches of orange.

'Will you be in trouble?' he asked, skirting the outer walls of the enclosure and drawing up before the front door.

'Probably. Don't worry about it,' she said. 'It's no new state for me to be in!'

'Didn't your namesake have the same problem?'

'Who? Oh, Jeanne d'Arc! I don't really think you can compare the two. Mother Dorothy certainly won't have me burned at the stake.'

'Is that you, Petrie?' Detective Sergeant Mill had wound down the window to address the figure looming out of the encircling whiteness.

'Yes, sir.' The young constable bent to peer in. 'The pony's safe in her stall. Good evening, Sister! Not illegally parking anywhere today?'

'Thanks awfully for reminding me!' Sister Joan said bitterly as she alighted from the passenger seat. 'I'd forgotten all about it, and then I wouldn't have made a full and perfect general confession! Did Sister Teresa give you some tea?'

'Indeed she did, Sister. Home baked scones with jam and cream too. Very tasty!'

'I'll be in touch,' Detective Sergeant Mill said, as his constable got into the car.

She lifted her hand and went in, noticing that the front door had been left ajar. From the antechamber leading to the parlour Mother Dorothy called, 'Close the front door, Sister, and come in here for a moment, please!'

' "Will you come into my parlour",' Sister Joan muttered under her breath, closing the heavy door and stepping to the left. 'Good evening, Mother Prioress. I'm afraid I was delayed.'

'But not it seems without due cause,' Mother Dorothy said judiciously. 'I understand from Constable Petrie that a young woman has been murdered over on the industrial estate, and that you knew her.'

'I only met her once,' Sister Joan said. 'She worked for a telephone answering firm, and I wished to make enquiries concerning someone who was offering to remove unwanted scrap metal etcetera from old houses. She'd never met the gentleman and his estimate was too high anyway.'

'A very neat précis of what I suspect is a very much longer story. Come into the parlour, Sister.'

Said the spider to the fly.

In the parlour she knelt for the greeting that was never omitted, and stood, not having been invited to take one of the stools, while Mother Dorothy put the flat-topped desk between them, tilting the lamp on it so that its beam fell on Sister Joan's face.

We have ways of making you talk, Sister Joan thought, and choked back a nervous giggle.

'In the past,' Mother Dorothy said, 'you have helped out in certain investigations. This I allowed because we are all bound to serve the ends of truth and justice. I must confess that I am anxious at the ease with which you appear to become involved in such matters. No, I don't require to be told that it's not your fault. It begins to look as if part of your *raison d'être* is to assist in such investigations from time to time. However you must guard against neglecting your spiritual life and you must remember that your present task is to clear out those storerooms. Should anything be found there worth the selling that will help our present financial situation very greatly. I have a question to ask you.'

'Yes, Mother Dorothy?'

'In view of the fact that you are now apparently helping the police again do you feel able to make full confession before your sisters today?'

'Not without going into a lot of irrelevant detail, Mother.'

'In that case you will retain your seat during confession and leave the matter to me. You will accept the penance imposed?'

'Yes, Mother Prioress.'

'Thank you, Sister.' For the first time her superior smiled, its warmth transcending the austere countenance. 'What is that under your arm?'

'It's an album of Victorian photographs, Mother. It came originally from this house, and it was thought that—'

'Take it up to the library before you take your place in chapel. Sister David will like to see it as well. *Dominus vobiscum.*'

'*Et cum spiritu tuo.*'

Sister Joan knelt briefly and went ahead of the prioress into the chapel passage.

The rest of the community were already in their places, save for Sister Hilaria and Bernadette. The novice mistress made her own general confession privately to Mother Prioress while Bernadette, as postulant, made hers to Mother Hilaria and was not expected until she became a novice proper to humble herself before the rest. It was humbling too, Sister Joan thought, going up the spiral staircase at the side of the Lady Altar, to have to stand up and confess all the trifling little faults which, tiny in themselves, blotted the perfection of the living rule.

In the library she switched on the lamp, laid the photograph album on top of one of the low bookcases, then abruptly changed her mind and thrust it in among a pile of old Latin missals where it was completely inconspicuous. She made a mental note to show the book to Sister David and went down the stairs again, taking her place as Mother Dorothy entered.

'Let us make a good confession, my daughters.'

Mother Dorothy dealt with sin as briskly as she dealt with anything else. The nuns rose, voices chiming together, 'I confess to You, oh Lord, to you, my sisters, that I have sinned exceedingly, through my fault, through my fault, through my most grievous fault—'

Clenched fists beat softly on modestly confined breasts. This was a cleansing process.

'Sit.' Mother Dorothy inclined her head and took her own seat.

The space before the altar was empty, waiting for the first penitent. There was the usual pause before Sister Gabrielle, giving the lead as usual, rose and made her way, stick tapping, to what Sister Teresa had nicknamed the hot seat.

'I confess to you, my sisters, that I have fallen asleep twice this week during morning meditation,' she said. 'I also confess Sister Perpetua for failing to wake me up.'

'Perhaps Sister Perpetua was about to confess that herself, Sister Gabrielle,' Mother Dorothy said.

'I was not, Mother Prioress.' Sister Perpetua stood up in her place. 'I don't regard it as a fault to allow an elderly lady to enjoy a brief nap wherever she happens to be!'

'It was an omission, Sister Perpetua. I believe our Lord would regard it as such. Didn't He reproach His friends when they failed to watch with Him in the Garden of Gethsemane?' Mother Dorothy said.

'May the Lord's Will be done.' Sister Perpetua sat down.

'Was there anything else, Sister Gabrielle?' The prioress glanced at her.

'I also confess to a lack of charity,' Sister Gabrielle said. 'Sister Perpetua left me to snore on with the best intentions.'

'The road to Hell is paved with them so we are told. Was there anything else?'

'No, Mother.'

'Sister Perpetua? Do you wish to make your confession now?'

Sister Perpetua exchanged places with Sister Gabrielle.

'I confess to you, my sisters, that I have been short-tempered this week.'

Sister Perpetua always confessed to a short temper. Sister Joan's attention wandered. If the public had to stand up once a week and confess all their little faults, all their meannesses and omissions of virtue to their neighbours, would society improve? And how many angels could dance on the point of a pin? The question was irrelevant. Perhaps the whole ritual was irrelevant – this catalogue of shabby little faults admitted by a group of semi-cloistered women when, on a cold slab in the morgue, a nice, ordinary girl lay dead, strangled, and a couple of shocked and grieving parents made ready to travel down and identify her.

'Sister Gabrielle, for your penance, watch and wait for two hours in the chapel here between midnight and five in the morning,' Mother Dorothy was saying. 'Sister Perpetua, since you lack patience, perhaps you may learn it by absenting yourself from recreation for two evenings next week and cleaning the brasses.'

Jane Sinclair had looked through the album and the next day had phoned up and asked for a meeting. She had been in the habit of gazing through the landing window of her flat into the old churchyard. She had mentioned Grant Tarquin and resurrection. There had been halfprints in the dust around the tombs, the one tomb medieval, the other a modern reproduction.

'Since Sister Joan is helping the authorities with an investigation she feels unable to make a full confession at this time.' Mother Dorothy was speaking again. 'She has kindly empowered me with the task of setting her a penance. I know that she has wasted money unnecessarily this week so she will be pleased to donate the remaining portion of her pocket money until the New Year to the missions. God's Will be done.'

'God's Will be done,' Sister Joan echoed.

If the poor were truly blessed, she thought wryly, then she was surely the most blessed sister in the Order.

Six

During supper – tomato and courgette pie with mashed potatoes and a syrup sponge pudding – and thank God for Sister Teresa who was a splendid little cook – Sister Joan tried to fix her attention upon the reading. It was the legend of some obscure child saint who sounded like the most appalling little prig. Her mind, however, flitted away to the afternoon's events. The old chapel with its tombs and the halfprints in the dust, Lilith's being cut free – for heaven's sake! that fact had gone clean out of her mind when Detective Sergeant Mill had informed her of Jane Sinclair's murder! Someone had cut the pony's rein, leaving her rider momentarily stranded in a misty graveyard with its leaning headstones and long grass. That meant someone had seen her go into the cemetery, had hidden, then when she was looking at Grant Tarquin's grave, had cut the rein and led Lilith silently along the grass verge to the road.

A chill ran down her back as she tried not to contemplate what might have happened if the detective hadn't arrived. She wondered if Detective Sergeant Mill had properly taken in what she had told him about someone having cut the rein. Probably he had tucked it away for future reference but his conscious attention had been on Jane Sinclair and her death.

The reading had ended without her hearing it. Presumably the priggish little horror had been gathered to the angels. Mother Dorothy smiled her thanks to Sister Martha.

'Very nicely read, Sister. The innocence of children is something we must all aspire to emulate. Sister Joan, next week you will be reading the book at suppertime, I believe? I think we would all enjoy hearing the story of Jeanne d'Arc again. Will you choose relevant extracts from one of her biographies?

Sister David has reached Jeanne d'Arc in her series of booklets for children so she will be glad to help you.'

'Yes, Mother Prioress.' Sister Joan bowed her head.

Not Marina Warner's work, she reflected as they rose for grace. Too intellectual and with an edge of scepticism which she personally relished but wouldn't have suited everybody. She'd be on safer ground with the biography that Vita Sackville-West had written.

'I'll be happy to help you, Sister,' Sister David whispered as they filed into the recreation room. 'You're going to be very busy clearing out the storerooms and helping the police. You are helping them again, aren't you?'

'Only in a very minor way,' Sister Joan murmured back. 'I'll be glad of your help with Jeanne d'Arc though. I'll get the extracts marked tomorrow afternoon.'

'Sister Joan and Sister David, Sister Martha needs help with winding her wool and Sister Katherine would like a partner for a game of Scrabble,' Mother Dorothy said, frowning slightly.

Sister Joan sat down at once reaching for the skeins of wool and giving Sister David the chance of a game. It wasn't an entirely selfless choice since while winding the wool she could allow her thoughts to roam and Sister Martha was unlikely to distract her with chatter.

There was a pattern running through recent events, beginning with her telling Luther that she'd been deputed to clear out the storerooms. Luther had chattered about it and someone – Mr Monam? had listened and acted very fast, having the circular printed and thrusting it through the convent door, registering with the telephone answering service and getting the estimate into the filing cabinet. Mr Monam then worked very swiftly and Mr Monam didn't want to be seen. She spread out her hands for a second skein of wool and thought about the footprints, the photograph with its chilling words scrawled across the back, Jane Sinclair's desire to meet her. The meeting had never happened because Miss Sinclair had received a telephone call that had sent her to the office earlier than usual, and someone had killed her there. Yes, of course! The man who had telephoned had broken into the office and then rung up, saying what? – 'Miss Sinclair? This is the police. Can you come to the office at once. There's been a break in here and we require you to check if anything's been taken. No, don't mention it to anyone. We're already following a lead' – something like that anyway! And Jane Sinclair had hurried off to the office and met her killer. She would have seen the broken lock and gone in unsuspectingly. It had to have been Mr Monam, whoever Mr Monam was. Jane Sinclair had never met him. He could have impersonated a plain-clothes officer, asked her to check the contents of the filing cabinet, stepped up behind her and—

The bell rang to signify the end of recreation. Sister Martha was putting the balls of newly wound wool into a bag, Sister David putting away the Scrabble board, the others rising, the light hum of conversation stilled.

They filed down to the chapel for the recitation of the rosary and the blessing that heralded the grand silence. She set aside further contemplation on the problem and let her thoughts and her fingers travel through the beads and the traditional prayers, her mind quietening as it always did.

Mother Dorothy with Sister David at her side stood ready to sprinkle each sister with holy water and utter the final blessing of the day. Sister Gabrielle had remained in her place, obviously preparing to keep her vigil and get the penance over with.

Sister Joan knelt, crossed herself and went out into the hall. Sister Teresa and Sister Marie were tying on their cloaks ready for the walk through the grounds to the postulancy where they now slept; Sister Hilaria joined them with Bernadette tagging at her heels, The others were mounting the staircase to their separate cells.

Sister Joan began her rounds. The windows had to be checked, the doors bolted, Alice coaxed into her basket, the stabledoor bolted. Lilith omitted her usual whinny and tossed her head irritably, evidently blaming Sister Joan for letting her loose on a main road with terrifying vehicles roaring past. The night was very still, the mist now blanket thick.

Sister Perpetua, a blanket over her arm, nodded towards the chapel wing. Yes, of course! Old Sister Gabrielle would appreciate a blanket while she was doing her penance in the cold chapel. Sister Joan took the blanket and went back down the corridor.

Sister Gabrielle sat in her place with the sanctuary lamp haloing her head. Eighty-six years old and as tough as well-seasoned leather, Sister Joan thought affectionately as she proffered the blanket, at the same time pointing to her watch and shaking her head slightly. It wanted nearly two hours to midnight before Sister Gabrielle's vigil was due to begin. The old lady nodded, grinned and allowed the blanket to be tucked round her. Evidently she'd decided to stay where she was.

Sister Joan went back down the corridor, slid the bolt into place on the connecting door, and hesitated. Sister Gabrielle couldn't spend the night locked up in the chapel wing! She might require the toilet or feel ill. On the other hand it wasn't wise to leave the connecting door unlocked. Mother Dorothy hadn't thought of that when she'd trotted out the penance.

Of course Mother Dorothy had thought of it! She had simply assumed that Sister Joan, being the one who locked up, would use her initiative and keep vigil as well. Sister Joan sent a brief yearning thought towards her empty bed and went back into the chapel. Unfortunately Sister Gabrielle was equally strong minded, frowning ferociously when she beheld the younger nun and making shooing signals with her hand. She clearly didn't relish being considered too old to stay alone in the chapel. Sister Joan made an apologetic gesture and headed for the library. At least she could take a look at the old photograph album to while away the time.

It was where she had left it. She pulled it out, switched on the overhead light over the desk and sat down. Sister David's notes on the booklet she was writing lay in a transparent folder on the desk top.

Jeanne d'Arc was a poor girl save in things of the spirit. All she had apart from the clothes she had borrowed and the armour that was made for her were two rings her family had given her, and the sword that the Archangel Michael had left for her to find.

Sister Joan slid the folder into the door and opened the photograph album. Something in it, she was certain, had attracted Jane Sinclair's attention, caused her to seek that meeting at the coffee shop.

The photographs were sepia-coloured, the ones in the first

pages faded almost to white so that it was hard to distinguish features. There were small groups of people seated on stools with others standing behind. Caps and aprons were much in evidence. Several photographs were of small children, standing stiffly on large chairs, wearing sailor-collared tunics and long curls. They could've been boys or girls, she thought, turning the pages slowly. Here a young man in a striped blazer with his hair parted in the middle held a tennis racquet awkwardly, while a young woman with her hair rolled up into an elaborate fringe looked at him apprehensively as if she wasn't sure whether he was going to hit the ball or her. In the background a potted palm looked entirely out of place.

Later photographs were more sharply defined and slightly less posed. Here and there a hand was blurred as the sitter had moved impatiently. One showed a young girl who had her back half turned to reveal a bustled skirt and was smiling over her shoulder. There were captions under some of the pictures but the ink had faded and the light in the library wasn't strong enough to decipher them. She turned the pages more slowly, stopping abruptly as a face leapt out at her.

Smiling, arrogant, dark brows winged above dark eyes, Grant Tarquin gazed out at her. No, it couldn't be the Grant Tarquin who had died the previous year. It had to be his father or grandfather. The open-necked shirt with the cravat tucked in at the throat could have been worn at any period.

Was this what Jane Sinclair had seen? Why should it have aroused her interest? Sister Joan closed the book. There was no evidence that Jane Sinclair's desire to meet her had had anything at all to do with the album anyway! She hadn't mentioned it. She'd mentioned Grant Tarquin and the cemetery and resurrection.

From down in the chapel there came a sudden inarticulate cry. She sprang up and ran down the spiral staircase into the chapel, her heart in her mouth. One glance told her that Sister Gabrielle wasn't in her seat. Only the blanket trailed from the carved end of the pew.

'Sister!' Raising her voice, she rushed into the corridor. The outside door at the end was open, the cold white mist drifting in like snow.

'Missed him!'

Sister Gabrielle appeared like a wraith in the doorway, her walking stick raised.

'Sister Gabrielle, are you all right?' Sister Joan hurried to offer her arm which was impatiently shaken off.

'Shut the door, child!' Sister Gabrielle said briskly. 'I'm perfectly all right. The young lad will have a bad headache in the morning though. I caught him full on the bridge of his nose. Probably broke it!'

'I'm bolting the outer door,' Sister Joan said firmly. 'Nobody will want to come and pray here tonight in this fog and, if they do, they'll just have to knock, that's all! Sister, you'd better come through to the kitchen and I'll make you some tea. Do you need a doctor?'

'Of course I don't need a doctor,' Sister Gabrielle said. 'A cup of tea with a slug of brandy in it would be welcome though.'

'Shall I call Mother Dorothy? We've broken the grand silence.'

'Which in emergency is permitted. Leave Mother Dorothy to her rest. I'll have that tea.'

They went through into the main part of the house, Sister Joan bolting the connecting door. She was rewarded with a snort from the older nun.

'The horse,' said Sister Gabrielle, 'has bolted. Come along, and don't disturb Sister Mary Concepta. She'll only fuss and flap.'

They went softly past the infirmary door into the kitchen. Alice slept peacefully, serenely unaware that she was supposed to be a guard dog.

'Sit down, Sister. I'll make the tea,' Sister Joan said.

'Make one for yourself,' Sister Gabrielle said, lowering herself with a grunt into her chair. 'You look pale as milk, girl!'

There was never any joy in arguing with Sister Gabrielle. Sister Joan put the smaller kettle on and measured tea into the pot, took down mugs, added sugar and a dash of brandy.

'What happened, Sister Gabrielle?' she asked when they were seated at opposite sides of the table with their steaming drinks.

'I decided to stay behind in the chapel and keep vigil all night,' Sister Gabrielle said. 'More convenient than going out and coming back in at midnight. I was trying to pass my time in profitable thoughts, wondering if there was any way I could add to the convent's income instead of being a burden.'

'You couldn't be a burden,' Sister Joan began.

'Don't be sentimental, girl!' Sister Gabrielle scowled at her. 'Of course I'm a burden and so is Mary Concepta. We have the right to be a burden for heaven's sake! But the recession's hit everybody and we don't contribute anything practical any longer. And we both need feeding at regular intervals and heat. At our age you need a bit of warmth. Anyway I was racking my brains and getting nowhere when someone came into the chapel. Well, I was suspicious at once.'

'Why?' Sister Joan asked.

'Because he crept in so quietly,' Sister Gabrielle said. 'Oh, people are generally quiet when they come into a church, but there's a quietness that doesn't want to disturb and a quietness that doesn't want to be noticed. And on such a night who'd be coming all the way up here to pray in our chapel when they could pray in the church down town? So I was suspicious.'

'Did he attack you?'

'He didn't even see me at first,' Sister Gabrielle said with satisfaction. 'He came in and looked round, like someone who's never been in a church before. He didn't genuflect to the altar either so he wasn't a Catholic. And then he started creeping up the aisle.'

'On tiptoe?'

'No, just creeping along. He had rubber-soled tennis shoes on. Very dirty and wet through, and a long gaberdine mackintosh with the collar turned up and one of those knitted bobble caps pulled over his head. Anyway he suddenly saw me and as I stood up he made a lunge and I whacked him across the bridge of his nose. He gave a kind of muffled yell and then turned and went back into the passage. He was a bit dazed, I think, because I caught up with him at the door and gave him another whack. It only glanced off his arm, and then he ran off into the fog. And then you came along.'

'You should have called me,' Sister Joan reproached.

'If the day ever comes when I can't handle a silly young lad then I'll fold my hands and turn up my toes,' Sister Gabrielle said scornfully.

'We ought to telephone the police.'

'Now what good would it do to disturb them late at night when nothing was taken and the lad's long gone?' the other demanded reasonably. 'No, you can mention it to your detective friend when you see him next, but there's no point in upsetting everybody at this hour. And Mother Dorothy has enough on her mind, trying to figure out a way to keep a roof over our heads without fretting about intruders. That was a good cup of tea, Sister. You're a terrible cook but you do brew a decent cup of tea or coffee. I'd best get back into chapel.'

'You're surely not going to do your penance now!' Sister Joan exclaimed.

'It's got to be done sooner or later. Better sooner. And you will take yourself off to bed! Nobody is going to get into the chapel again tonight, not with the outer door bolted. I'll unlock it first thing in the morning when I'm done praying. Now don't argue with me!'

'I wouldn't dare,' Sister Joan said with an unwilling grin.

'Right then!' Sister Gabrielle rose heavily. 'We'll stop chattering now. The emergency is over and we've no licence to gossip. Goodnight, Sister.'

'Goodnight, Sister Gabrielle.'

Sister Joan remained at the table, her hands cupped round her cooling mug. She felt too wrought up to sleep, her senses tuned to a finer pitch than usual. With the outer door locked Sister Gabrielle would be free from intrusion, but somewhere out there in the cold, white, clinging mist was the intruder whom Sister Gabrielle had set about with her walking stick. A lad, she had termed him. That didn't sound like Grant Tarquin. Neither could she picture Grant Tarquin in a long gaberdine and a bobble hat.

But Grant Tarquin was dead. He had died, unmarried and unmourned, more than a year before. She had stood by his grave that same afternoon. And Jane Sinclair was dead too. Strangled before she could confide her worries to a sympathetic ear.

She rose, rinsed the cups and gave Alice a last pat before she went upstairs. Only the dimmed lights burned on the upper landing. On the left a narrow passage divided rooms that had been divided into cells with two bathrooms at the end. She went into her own cell and switched on the light, an extravagance she would have to confess the following week. Sisters coming late to bed for whatever reason were supposed to undress in the dark. At this moment, however, she needed to look round her small domain, fill her eyes with its comfortable familiarity.

The room was ten feet square, its walls whitewashed with only a small, wooden cross on one of them. A small window with wooden shutters that lay flat against the inner wall at each side had a plain white blind which when raised allowed a view over the stable yard. An iron-framed bed held a thin mattress, grey blankets and a large pillow. A shelf on one wall held her missal, her spiritual diary, a life of her patron saint. The bare bulb in the ceiling shed lustre on the bowl and jug on the floor with her toothbrush and toothpaste. The bathrooms were for the twice weekly bath with the water only heated for nuns over the age of sixty. More than twenty years to go, she thought, with an amused twitch of the lips. Her outer garments hung on hooks and a locker with two drawers held her underwear and had on its plain deal surface a plain glass jar with some late sprays of heather in it.

'You'll never stand the life!' Jacob had mocked when she had finally told him that she couldn't become a Jew and marry him. 'All right, so don't marry me! But don't fool yourself into celibacy either. Go off and marry someone else but don't deny the rest of your life in a quest for martyrdom!'

Darling Jacob with his keen, dark Semitic face and incisive wit corroding into bitterness because he was as trapped in his own culture as she was in hers. It had been hard in the beginning. Even now she found traces of Jacob in many of the men she met – in Detective Sergeant Mill, in the brief acquaintanceship she had had with Grant Tarquin.

Grant Tarquin. He was dead and his forebears were dead, but someone had tiptoed round the tombs in the old chapel, tiptoed up and down the aisles between the piled boxes in the storerooms. And someone had written that sentence across the back of the photograph hidden in the roll of motheaten brocade. 'We have a secret, the Devil and I.'

Against such sentiments the cell was a defence, a reminder that purity and order could still prevail. She began to undress, removing fob watch and narrow belt to which her rosary was attached, unpinning the neat white scapular which confined the grey bodice of her anklelength habit, unpinning the short white veil and letting her crop of blue-black curls spring free. Under the habit she was still wearing her jeans, having forgotten to remove them. Another fault, she reflected, and grimaced.

The light out she slid between the rough blankets, wishing for the thousandth time that nuns were permitted to wear pyjamas and bedsocks. The long, straight, Victorian nightgown catapulted her into a previous century just as the rule itself kept alive a medieval routine. Past and present were inextricably combined.

The past lay in the storerooms. She had known that from the beginning. Someone was anxious to find something there before she did. But who? And what was hidden? The second question was easier to answer than the first. Clearly something of great value had been left there among all the rubbish, the flotsam and jetsam of more than 200 years. Something small, she guessed, lying flat on her back and staring up at the ceiling. Jewellery? Wouldn't jewellery have been removed before the estate was sold? A manuscript of some kind? The Tarquins were an old family. The Sir Richard Tarquine whose tomb was in the old chapel in the cemetery had fought in the Hundred Years' War, and died peacefully in his own bed. All the Tarquins slept peacefully now, scattered through the burying ground. None of them walked above ground. Yet when she slept at last she dreamed of Grant Tarquin tiptoeing through the silent house.

Seven

Sunday was an oasis at the beginning of the week. There was a tranquillity that ran like a thread through the day, binding hour to hour. After the prayers and the high mass of the morning there was leisure – to study privately, to walk in the garden, to read and write letters and do all the things for which the rest of the week held no space. This morning it was Father Malone who officiated at mass, his homely Irish brogue investing the words with Celtic charm, the frayed hem of his cassock visible under the Advent surplice. The Host on the High Altar and the statue on the Lady Altar had been covered with purple to await the blaze of glory that was Christmas.

'This murder is a terrible thing now, wouldn't you say?'

He stood chatting to the sisters as they drank the Sunday morning cup of coffee in the dining-room.

Sister Joan repressed a smile. Father Stephens would have uttered mellifluous phrases about the world waiting for the Christ Child. Father Malone was more firmly earth anchored.

'Has there been one?' Sister Katherine asked.

'Have you not heard? I'd have thought Sister Joan would be in the thick of the investigations as usual!' He glanced towards her. 'I had it from the Reverend Jackson when he came round for a bit of a chat after supper. The poor girl was a Protestant, God rest her soul. Her parents are travelling down tomorrow to identify her officially and stay over for her funeral. Yes, strangled she was, in broad daylight on the industrial estate. It's a violent world we live in and no mistake! Of course, I asked him to let me know at once if there was anything I could do. The Reverend Jackson is a fine preacher. It's a pity he was reared in the wrong faith.'

'But surely Protestants will get to heaven too,' Sister David said, with a hint of mischief.

'All good living people who obey the Creator will enter heaven,' Father Malone said firmly. 'The only difference is that while the Jews and the Muslims and the Protestants have a long, weary walk to the golden gates we Catholics will whizz past them in a bus.'

'Who was murdered, Father?' Sister Martha asked.

'A Miss Sinclair. Jane Sinclair. Only twenty-two years old, and a nice, quiet girl by all accounts. Not a regular churchgoer more's the pity. However she probably hadn't been brought up to it. Many young people aren't these days. It's my belief that we should look nearer home when we start sending missions to the heathen. That industrial estate, now, takes the overflow from the council estate, but it's been thrown up in a hurry. Half the buildings are empty. And the rubbish in the streets you wouldn't believe. The Reverend Jackson and I have hopes of starting up a youth club, somewhere the young people can come to play records and ping-pong and find out that having a bit of crack means having a good gossip and not sticking a needle in your arm.'

'You're wasting your time, Father,' Sister Perpetua said bluntly. 'They'll tear any youth club down within a couple of weeks.'

'Ah now, Sister, that's a mite harsh!' he protested. 'There are some good people in every place. A lot of them just lack a focus, you know. They get rid of their energies by battering one another. Only this morning I saw a lad with a cut across his nose and a black eye lounging near the old town hall. You know the place I mean. It was turned into three good-sized houses when the council had the new town hall built.'

'Did you know the boy?' Sister Joan asked.

'Only by sight. He always waves and shouts something bold when he sees me. Not the way a good Catholic lad would behave but then he's not one of my flock and his noticing me at all might count for nothing or a very great deal – the Lord works in very mysterious ways!'

'You don't know where he lives?' Sister Joan persisted.

'He hangs out near one of the office complexes that've sprung up, Sister. If you're troubled about his injury it's a credit to your tender heart, but believe me, these young people bounce back like tennis balls. That can't be the time! Father Stephens will think I've been kidnapped. The problem is that I cannot tear myself away from such charming company!'

Sister Joan glanced at Sister Gabrielle who frowned and shook her head slightly. Evidently the previous night's events were not yet to be related.

The afternoon would give her the opportunity, she decided. First she'd work on the readings she was due to give during the coming week, and then she'd take Lilith for a ride.

At the chapel door Sister Gabrielle tugged at her sleeve, muttering out of the side of her mouth like some elderly gangster, 'Mother Dorothy has enough to worry her, Sister. We'll say nothing for the present.'

'Very well, Sister.'

'I'm going to have a little nap,' Sister Gabrielle said in her ordinary voice. 'I'm getting too old to sit up all day!'

She clumped back down the corridor. Sister Joan went up to the library.

The mist had cleared from the top of the moors but from the windows she could see long trails of thick white vapour swinging gently like sheets out to dry on the lower slopes. It was dim enough to require a light in order to see what she was doing. She sat down at the desk and opened the file in which Sister David was writing her account of the French saint.

'I've brought the translation of the trial for you to look at, Sister.'

Sister David came in, weighed down with volumes.

'Thank you, Sister. I have the Sackville-West biography in my own cell. Is it all right for me to use your notes?'

'Oh, please do! I'm delighted to think they may help out,' Sister David said at once. 'There's a Sackville-West here somewhere to save your using your own copy.'

She had glided to one of the tall bookcases and was on her knees. One day Sister David would find the time to update the catalogue in the library but Sister Joan wouldn't have cared to hazard a guess when.

'Oh, how interesting!' Sister David sat back on her heels. 'I didn't even know this was here! Look, a booklet about the Tarquins, Sister. They go back a long way, to the Crusades, I believe, though they say nowadays the Crusaders weren't as noble as I was taught to believe. The whole matter calls for some fresh research.'

Her face was bright at the prospect. People who declared that ink ran in Sister David's veins failed to realize that it was passionate ink. Other women dreamed of lovers or fame, while everything that wasn't concentrated in her spiritual life was focused by Sister David on dreams of dusty manuscripts in dead languages that might shine a torch into the darkness of the past.

'May I have a look at it later?' Sister Joan asked.

'I'll leave it here for you. I must go now and leave you in peace. I promised Sister Katherine to help her sort out the Christmas decorations. She likes to get them ready in plenty of time.'

Sister David vanished. Sister Joan glanced at the booklet, then heroically turned her attention back to the job in hand.

Her pen flew, making notes. She wanted to pick out anecdotes that made the saint more human – a tough young peasant with a salty wit who didn't spend all her time on her knees listening to voices or charging up and down a battlefield on a horse!

> *She called her friends by nicknames and liked to jest with them, but she wept often too over the cruelty of war and the sad state of the poor and dispossessed. She herself might have grown very rich after she had relieved Orleans and many gifts of money and horses were made to her. She bought herself some fine court clothes and gave all the rest to the poor. All she cared about were the banner she had made and the sword the Archangel Michael had given to her and the two rings, one gold engraved with the name of Jesu and one silver engraved with the name of Maria which her brothers had given to her, but when she was captured all those things were stolen from her and yet she still was rich in her faith.*

It was shaping very well, Sister Joan decided, laying out the bits of paper from which she could mark relevant passages. She'd been at it for over an hour and her back was aching.

'Sister, Mother Dorothy wants to know if you're taking Lilith out again today,' Sister David had reappeared.

'Yes. Did she wish to see me?'

'Only to remind you to take off your jeans when you got back,' Sister David said.

'Our prioress can see round corners, I'm convinced of it,' Sister Joan chuckled.

'How are you getting on?' Sister David came to the desk.

'Quite well. I've marked the extracts I want to read.'

'Would you like me to type them out for you, Sister, then you won't have to carry a pile of books up to the dining-room,' Sister David offered.

'It would be a great help but I don't want to put you to trouble,' Sister Joan began.

'It'll be a pleasure to do,' Sister David said with evident sincerity. 'Don't forget the booklet you wanted to read.'

'Thank you, Sister.'

Picking up the booklet Sister Joan went back to the main part of the house, and went up to her cell to put on her jeans. While smoothing the skirt of her habit down over them she found herself paying silent tribute to Mother Dorothy who, without any loss of face, had made it possible for her to ride down into town again and, if she wished, continue her investigations into a case of which nothing much had been confided to her. Mother Dorothy was showing her a considerable degree of trust. Sister Joan made up her mind to remember that the next time the prioress irritated her.

She had put the booklet on the shelf. Privately printed, she guessed, probably an attempt by someone with a sense of family to leave a modest record for posterity.

It was something to be looked at later. She reached for her cloak and went down to the stable where Lilith deigned to greet her with a whinny to mark another walk on the second successive day. There was no sign of Alice. Sister Joan guessed she was over at the postulancy cadging titbits.

Outside the air was still unseasonably mild. Mounting up she cantered past the walls that enclosed the garden and the little cemetery where past sisters of Cornwall House slept their last sleep and headed for the track that dipped down towards the council estate, with the industrial estate blotting the landscape beyond.

Father Malone had mentioned a lad with an injured nose and

a black eye. It was of course entirely possible that the injuries weren't due to Sister Gabrielle's walking stick but in her own experience stray remarks made in innocence usually led somewhere.

The old town hall had been turned into private dwelling places nearly fifteen years before but would always be known in local parlance as the old town hall. What were now three substantial houses were situated in a road that ran parallel to the main street that marked the demarcation between the council estate and the older part of the town. It was a pity that the old and the new couldn't be melded together with more taste, she mused, guiding Lilith across the road and dismounting.

A Sunday afternoon hush hung over the town, a hush intensified by the mist which wreathed and twisted about the corners of the buildings and distorted the faint chiming of bells from a nearby church. It was hardly likely that the lad with the facial injury would still be hanging about, she reflected, as she walked along the road. In any case he wasn't likely to admit that he'd sneaked into the convent chapel. Another thought struck her. Surely a mugger would have wrested the stick from Sister Gabrielle and pushed her to the ground. Sister Gabrielle was a tough old lady but an old lady for all that! Yet the lad had fled. A prospective thief with a conscience or one whose heart wasn't in his occupation?

A couple of girls came round the corner, both wearing jeans and bright tartan jackets. Friends, she surmised, who liked dressing in similar styles because they weren't yet confident in their own separate identities, lipstick expertly applied, eyes eager for experience.

'Don't worry about Lilith!' she called cheerfully, as they made to cross the road. 'She's over twenty years old and wouldn't hurt a fly!'

The girls hesitated, glancing at each other in an embarrassed fashion that made her feel amused and a little sad. It was clear that it wasn't only nervousness of the pony that had caused them to begin to swerve away. Some people seemed to think that religious vocations were infectious.

'Is that old for a horse?' one of the girls asked.

'Pretty middle-aged for some but horses are a bit like people,'

Sister Joan said pleasantly. 'They're as young as they feel. Now I'm seventy-three but you'd never guess it.'

'I bet you're not!' the other girl said and giggled.

'I'm nearly thirty-nine.'

There was a little silence, then the first girl said politely, 'You look awfully good for your age.'

'Thank you.' Sister Joan refrained from smiling. 'Do either of you ride or is it all motorbikes these days?'

'We don't ride motorbikes,' the taller of the girls said. 'Some of the boys do but we don't often get to go on them.'

'I daresay they're expensive to run,' Sister Joan nodded. 'You don't have a youth club or anything round here?'

'A youth club!' The younger of the two girls sounded as shocked as if Sister Joan had recommended a brothel. 'No, nothing like that. We watch telly and hang out down at the Casbah – that's a café. It's open on Sundays.'

'Is that where you're going now?'

She sensed a drawing back, a sudden trepidation that shivered between them.

'We're on our way home,' the older girl said firmly. 'We live next to each other. We ought to hurry, Patsy. Your mum'll be fretting.'

'You live in Cemetery Road?'

They had been coming away from the housing estate.

'I'm sorry,' said the one who wasn't named Patsy, 'but we're not supposed to talk to strangers, not with—' She had broken off abruptly and her companion finished the sentence.

'That strangler around. Mrs Dalton was telling my mum all about it. Awful it was.'

'My name's Sister Joan. I'm from Cornwall House.'

'Anyone can say that,' Patsy said with a hint of truculence. 'Anyone can dress up as a nun and go round strangling people.'

'And make their getaway on an elderly pony?' Sister Joan grinned and then nodded. 'You're right. It's best to be safe and go everywhere together until he's caught. I heard there was another person attacked last night – a boy?'

The two girls looked at each other.

'She means Jeb,' said the one who wasn't named Patsy. 'D'ya know Jeb?'

'If he siphons petrol out of vans and then charges for guarding the vehicle while the owner goes off to buy some more petrol, then I know Jeb,' Sister Joan said wryly.

'That's Jeb!' Patsy giggled. 'Right little bugg – beggar Jeb is! Fancy you knowing him.'

'I only met him once,' Sister Joan said. 'He seems very nice.'

'Nice?' Patsy looked at her doubtfully. 'He's OK I suppose.'

'I was hoping he wasn't too badly hurt,' Sister Joan said.

'I don't think so.'

'Would you happen to know where he lives?'

'He's got a squat somewhere behind the old town hall. Comes and goes.'

'Thanks. I might pay a call on him.'

She turned Lilith's head towards the narrow entry that ran down the side of the converted houses.

'Will you be all right by yourself?' Patsy said suddenly with a rather touching motherly air.

'I'll be fine honestly,' Sister Joan said. 'God bless now!'

She was further touched to hear them muttering the salutation in an embarrassed fashion before they bounced off together.

The road that ran behind the old town hall ended in a cul-de-sac. To the left gates hung askew at the entrance to a large, overgrown garden which fronted a detached two-storey house. Sister Joan stood at the broken gates and looked at the building with a considering eye. It was a modern house despite the creeper that crept over the walls and the trees that shielded the windows from the light. Several of the windows were cracked and there were some tiles missing from the roof. It looked neglected, sad.

'It could very well be a squat,' Sister Joan said to Lilith and guided the pony on to the long grass, tethering her loosely to the branch of a lilac tree that leaned out, crooked and unpruned, from the hedge.

She walked on up to the front door and lifted the greeny-bronze knocker two or three times, disturbing a small colony of bats that rose and circled about the roof, their wings dipping in and out of the hanging sheets of mist.

Sister Joan, mindful that she ought to love all God's creatures, loved bats *in absentia*, and hastily gave the door a hefty shove which precipitated her into a hall with a staircase opposite and the open doors of a long drawing-room on the left. Her hand felt for a switch and a light sprang into being. Obviously nobody had bothered to turn off the electricity.

The floors were bare of carpets but the odd items of furniture that stood about were of good quality. She crossed to the double doors and looked in. The curtains at the bay windows were closed and the big room had a spare unused aspect.

'Jeb! Jeb, are you here? It's Sister Joan!'

Standing in the middle of the hall again, calling, she felt her voice bounce back at her from the bare walls. There was no other sound.

At the right a door opened into an L-shaped room which curved round into a kitchen. Switching on lights as she went she walked through and looked at the grease-stained cooker, the sink which held a couple of dirty cups, the curling crust of a piece of toast on the table. In the refuse bin in the corner were a couple of coke tins and the remains of a packet of crisps.

'Jeb!' Going out into the hall again, switching off the lights in an automatic habit of economy, she called more loudly.

Overhead something creaked. A floorboard settling for the evening? A cautious footfall?

'Jeb, there's nothing to worry about! I want a few words with you, that's all!' Switching on the stair light she went swiftly up the still carpeted treads on to the broad landing. It widened into an upper hall with doors around it.

The first door was open. She pushed it wider and almost fell over a large holdall placed just within. Regaining her balance she snapped on the light and looked round at the mattress and sleeping bag, the pile of disordered blankets. Jeb, if this was Jeb's squat, had made himself a kind of home here.

The next door resisted her efforts. It was either jammed or locked. She looked into the next room where a pile of rugs occupied most of the space, and into the fourth where several items of furniture, chairs and stools and occasional tables, were all jumbled up together. Jeb was clearly out. No doubt hustling and hawking his less than legal business in places like Nightingale Court. She thrust open the bathroom door, pulling the cord that operated the light switch, and stared at Jeb.

He sat on the floor with his back against the white enamel

bath, his head leaning back, his mouth slightly open. The mark across the bridge of his nose had paled and faded but the livid bruises on his throat were dark stains against the bloodless skin.

'I have to get out of here.'

She didn't realize she had spoken aloud until she saw in the mirror over the bath that her lips were moving and there was the sound of spoken words in her ears.

Backing out with infinite care, her cloak catching momentarily on the banisters as she turned, she wrenched it free and ran down the stairs and out through the front door. Some part of her expected the garden to be empty but Lilith was still grazing peacefully at the end of her tether.

Her fingers felt stiff and clumsy as she undid the rein and clambered up to the saddle. Then she was riding out on to the road again, urging Lilith down the darkening alley, turning on to the shop-bordered street that led into the main part of town.

The one or two people strolling along the pavement turned startled faces as she cantered past. At the police station the lights had been turned on and the illuminated blue sign over the entrance glowed reassuringly.

'Sister Joan, is something wrong up at the convent?'

Constable Petrie who was on desk duty looked up in concern as she ran in.

'There's a body in the house behind the old town hall,' Sister Joan said and sat down abruptly on the only available chair.

Constable Petrie was still in his twenties but had already attained the poker face of the traditional copper. Now his professional calm was distinctly ruffled.

'A body?' he said. 'Sister, are you sure?'

'Of course I'm sure! His name is Jeb. I don't think he mentioned his second name. He's in the bathroom.'

'I'll ring Detective Sergeant Mill. Excuse me, Sister.'

He retreated to the back of the space behind the desk, lifted the telephone, dialled and spoke rapidly. Sister Joan put her head briefly between her knees and fought an unpleasant wave of dizziness.

'I'll get you a cup of tea, Sister. Would you like to wait in the office? It's more private there. I'm looking after the shop by myself so to speak. You don't expect murder on a Sunday, do you?'

She went into the office and sat down, forcing herself to breathe deeply and evenly. She had seen violent death before but nothing in the world would ever accustom her to the experience or obliterate the sick, helpless rage which swept through her when she observed a human life cut short before due time.

'Here you are, Sister! Drink it while it's hot.' He put the mug down on the table. 'Detective Sergeant Mill will be here directly. He went home for a couple of hours to snatch a meal. We're still investigating the death of Jane Sinclair as you know.'

Odd, she thought irrelevantly, sipping the hot, syrupy brew. Alan Mill had a house and a wife and two children and she had never even enquired where he lived. She had never seen his wife or met his boys. Her contact with him was purely professional. Had it been any other way she would have had to withdraw. Helping the police was one thing. Personal friendships were something else.

'Has anything further come to light?'

'Not much, Sister. The poor girl seems to have lived a very quiet life. Nothing in her past to suggest she ever made a single enemy. Of course we'll get whoever did it. I don't suppose you noticed—?'

'The boy had been strangled,' Sister Joan said.

'Like Jane Sinclair.' His face quickly concealed shock. 'Oh dear, I hope we don't have a serial killer on our hands.'

Sister Joan was silent, privately doubting it. Jane Sinclair had been killed for a very specific reason, she was sure, as had Jeb. What those reasons were and how they were connected would give them the name of the murderer.

'Would you like me to ring the convent and let them know you might be a bit late back?' Constable Petrie was asking.

'That would be very kind of you, Constable.'

Being late was becoming a besetting fault, she thought wryly. Certainly Mother Dorothy would expect a fuller explanation of what was going on than she had so far received and when she'd heard it – Sister Joan privately thanked her stars that it wasn't possible to be relegated to the status of postulant!

A car drew up outside, brakes squealing slightly, and Detective Sergeant Mill strode past the office window. The set of his jaw looked grim. Sister Joan finished her tea and stood up.

'Petrie tells me you've found a body, Sister!'

He came in without greeting.

'Good afternoon, Detective Sergeant Mill. Yes, in the empty house behind the old town hall.'

'Right! We'll talk on the way. Did you know the victim?'

'Not really. His name's Jeb. When I first went to Nightingale Court to make some enquiries about the man who'd put the circular through the door the petrol was siphoned out of my van. When I came out he was hanging about. He offered to keep an eye on the van while I went to the nearest garage to get a can of petrol.'

'For a consideration, I daresay?'

They were at the car and he held open the door for her.

'Of course. I think he'd got a nice little racket going actually. But there was no harm in him. He didn't deserve—'

She bit her lip staring through the window at the street as the lights came on, mitigating the early darkness.

'Petrie's rounding up the doctor and the photographer,' Detective Sergeant Mill told her. 'I wanted to have a preliminary look with a material witness.'

'Me,' she said, in a small voice.

'Let's hope we haven't got a serial killer on the loose.' He echoed Constable Petrie's sentiments gloomily.

They had turned into the alley. Now wasn't the time to begin long explanations, she decided.

'What was the boy doing here, I wonder?'

At the broken gate he paused to stare at the ivy-clad façade.

'He was squatting here,' Sister Joan said. 'I brought Lilith out for a ride and met a couple of teenage girls who knew him slightly.'

'You were looking for him?'

'I was hoping I might run into him,' she admitted.

'Well, you seem to have done. This place belongs to the council now, I suppose, though they haven't paid much attention to it. Of course Grant Tarquin hardly ever lived there.'

'This was Grant Tarquin's property?'

'Didn't you know?' He glanced at her.

'I knew he built himself a house when his father died after the old gentleman sold the family estate to our Order. I assumed he left the district.'

'He did but he came back occasionally, paid his council tax and water rates and so on, and there's no law says a man has to live in his own house. Mind you don't touch anything, Sister – though I daresay you already did.'

'Only the light switches and door handles. He's upstairs in the bathroom. Do you mind if I stay down here?'

'No, of course not.'

He took the stairs two at a time. She stood in the hall, listening to his footsteps on the bare boards above, the snapping on of lights. Curiously the lights only threw into greater prominence the emptiness of the place.

'Sister Joan, will you come up here for a moment?' Detective Sergeant Mill had reappeared on the landing.

Reluctantly she ascended the stairs. Two pairs of eyes were more efficient than one when there might be clues to notice, but it wasn't pleasant to have to push aside shock and pity and look objectively at someone who had died violently.

The bathroom was empty, basin and floor shining in a way she was certain they hadn't shone before.

'Your body seems to have walked,' the detective said.

'That's not possible! He was here, sitting on the floor with his back against the bath and his head back. I saw the marks on his throat.'

The detective gave her a considering look and nodded.

'Yes, of course he was here,' he said. 'I've never known you to start hallucinating. The point is that there's nobody here now. You're sure he was dead and not just playing a rather cruel joke on you?'

'That makes no sense. He didn't know that I was looking for him.'

'Then someone moved him.'

'And wiped the floor and the basin afterwards,' she pointed out. 'I don't think they were this clean before.'

'Someone was in the house?'

'I don't know. I looked into the rooms but I didn't search them thoroughly. It's possible, I suppose. They'd have had time while I went to the police station and Constable Petrie telephoned you.'

'It might be on the premises still. Sister, there's nothing you can do here for the moment. I'll get a squad car to run you back to the convent.'

'I can ride Lilith,' she began.

'Not unescorted you won't,' he said grimly. 'Until we find this joker you'll make sure you stay where there's company. That's an order, Sister!'

Eight

Riding back to the convent, with the headlamps of the police car trailing her, she felt not safer but like a mischievous child being chased by a truant officer. In this case the officer was the stolid desk sergeant whose name she couldn't remember and who, to judge by the alacrity he turned at the gates and sped back the way he had come, had little liking for either convents or nuns on horseback.

She stabled Lilith, hurried upstairs to remove her jeans, and came down into the main hall to find Mother Dorothy talking to Detective Sergeant Mill.

'I'm being told you are being an invaluable help to the police,' the former said in a tone of unexpected amiability. 'I will not, of course, ask for any details at this stage, but Detective Sergeant Mill has a few questions to ask you. You have twenty minutes before benediction, Sister. You may use my parlour.'

'Thank you, Mother Prioress,' Sister Joan said.

'I'll have Sister Teresa bring you some tea since you've missed yours, Sister,' Mother Dorothy said, heroically refraining from adding the word "again". 'Did you make any headway with your preparations for the reading next week?'

'A great deal, Mother. Sister David has been very helpful,' Sister Joan said. When she and Detective Sergeant Mill were seated in the parlour with the tea, carried in by a Sister Teresa obviously bursting with curiosity, on the desk between them, he opened his notebook, unscrewed his pen, and lifting a dark eyebrow at her asked, 'What reading would that be, Sister?'

'At supper we take it in turns, week and week about, to read aloud from an improving book,' she explained. 'Next week's my turn.'

'At the risk of being snubbed,' he said amused, 'which improving book are you going to entertain the community with?'

'The story of my own patron saint, using extracts from various biographies and the text of her trial.'

'Well, at least you have something in common,' he said. 'You both ride around on horses—'

'Sticking our noses into what doesn't concern us. I know.'

'I was going to say setting the world to rights. However, let's not digress. The body you reported seems to have disappeared.'

'Aren't you looking for it?'

'On a foggy Sunday afternoon with only a skeleton staff on duty we've sufficient on hand with investigating into the murder of Jane Sinclair,' he said. 'Don't worry. We've locked up the house and left a man on duty there and tomorrow morning we'll start looking for the lad. That means knocking on doors, finding out about him – he doesn't seem to have any kind of criminal record, by the bye – and hopefully he'll turn up safe and sound or the converse. What I'd like to know from you is how you got involved in all this. Why were you looking for Jeb?'

'To ask him why he broke into the chapel last night.'

'What!' His glance sharpened. 'You didn't mention that before!'

'You didn't ask me. Detective Inspector, please keep your voice down. Nobody except Sister Gabrielle and I know that anyone did break in. We judged it better not to tell Mother Dorothy because she's got enough on her mind at the moment with trying to balance the books.'

'You and Sister Gabrielle were in the chapel when Jeb broke in?'

'Sister Gabrielle was. She had a vigil to keep there. I was up in the library, starting my Jeanne d'Arc preparations. I heard a muffled cry and ran down into the chapel. Sister Gabrielle told me a lad had crept in and she hit him across the nose with her walking stick and then followed him when he ran out.'

'How did she know it was Jeb?'

'She didn't, but this afternoon I took Lilith for a ride into town and met a couple of girls – one was called Patsy – and we fell into conversation. They were walking home together because they were nervous about the murder – they live next door to each other in Cemetery Road. One of them, I forget which, said it wasn't safe to go out these days, that they'd seen a boy they knew with a black eye and a cut on his nose earlier on hanging around, that his name was Jeb and he lived in a squat behind the old town hall.'

'I wish some of my men had your talent for gleaning information!' he said. 'I take it you knew this Jeb?'

'I'd met a Jeb,' she said carefully, 'when I went to the office in Nightingale Court to find out what I could about the circular that was pushed through my door, and when I came out someone had siphoned off all the petrol in the van. Then this boy turned up and offered to look after the van while I went to the garage – I told you all that.'

'Just getting it absolutely clear.' He made a note, put away pen and notebook, sat up straight, and said, 'This is off the record, Sister. Why did you ride Lilith down into the town a second day in succession?'

'I wanted to have another look in the cemetery,' she said.

'Why this sudden interest in graves? You're not usually so morbid.'

'Because I wanted to make sure that Grant Tarquin is really dead.'

'Why on earth should you think he isn't?' he demanded, in astonishment.

'Because I found the photograph of his grandfather – or great grandfather, with "We have a secret, the Devil and I", written on it, up in the storeroom,' she said levelly. 'And then I found footprints in the dust up there, half prints as if someone had been tiptoeing up and down the aisles. It was Sister David who remarked that devil worshippers went on tiptoe in consecrated ground, and, of course, this entire building has been, in a sense, consecrated. And then I couldn't find out who'd had the circular printed and put it through the door, and then Jane Sinclair telephoned me and said something about the cemetery so I rode Lilith down there and found the same footprints – I think you'll find Jeb's body there, in the old chapel in the cemetery!'

'Sister, if I were to put this in an official statement I'd be on traffic duty before you could blink!' he exclaimed. 'Devil worshippers, dead men or their grandfathers wandering about pushing circulars through doors – it's quite crazy, you know.'

'I don't think people do come out of their graves, of course I don't,' she said, 'but Grant Tarquin had a bad reputation when he was alive. He resented the fact that his father sold this estate so cheaply to our Order, and he went off leaving the house he'd built for himself empty. Is there proof that he really is dead? Jeb was found dead in his house after all.'

'Jeb wasn't found dead.'

'By me,' she said, her blue eyes level on his face.

'You think someone took the body – the alleged body – to the old cemetery. Why?'

'There were half footprints round the tombs in the little chapel of rest there,' she said, 'and while I was looking at Grant Tarquin's grave someone cut Lilith's rein and left me stranded. And before you say anything, no, I don't think Grant Tarquin or any of his forbears have risen from the dead, but I'd like to be sure it was Grant Tarquin they buried!'

'I haven't the slightest hope of getting an exhumation order and nor have I the slightest intention of applying for one,' he said.

'But you'll look in the old cemetery?'

'On my way home, and when I don't find anyone I'll continue on my way and spend the night watching television. Grant Tarquin is dead, Sister. Believe me.'

'As you say.' Rising with him, going ahead to open the door, she asked, 'Will Sister Gabrielle get into trouble? She was only defending herself.'

'I think we can leave Sister Gabrielle out of it.' His mouth relaxed into a smile. 'She's a formidable old girl, isn't she? There isn't anything worth stealing up in the storerooms, is there?'

'I doubt it. There are rolls of motheaten silk and brocade, some broken chairs, piles of old newspapers, books with the covers torn off – there might be something that can be recycled but that's all. Old Sir Robert Tarquin was generous enough to let our Order have the estate very cheaply but I really don't think he'd have left the family jewels up in the storerooms.'

'I think you're right. You know Alice should have given warning that a stranger was in the vicinity. She's proving a dead loss as a guard dog.'

'She's very young,' Sister Joan said. 'Give her time.'

As they came into the hall the ringing of the bell for benediction interrupted them.

'I'll be off then.' He moved to the door.

'You're welcome to stay and join us.'

'No thanks. I've another chapel to visit. Good evening to you, Sister.'

Frowning a little she closed the front door behind him and tagged into chapel behind Sister Martha.

She was on her way out of chapel when the telephone rang. A glance at Mother Dorothy, who nodded, and she sped into the kitchen passage to answer it.

'Sister Joan?'

'Speaking.'

'Alan Mill here. You were right, Sister. There's a body of a teenage boy, apparently strangled, in the chapel of rest in the old cemetery. I'm waiting for the squad car.'

'Do you need me?' she asked.

'Not yet. I may have to ask you to confirm it's the boy you spoke to in Nightingale Court but that can wait until tomorrow. I can send up a car for you after breakfast.'

'I'll get permission to drive in. Detective Sergeant, are there any footprints?'

'Just a series of scrapes in the dust, presumably where the body was dragged in. Mind, I only have my torch. I'm signing off now. The squad car's here.'

She heard the little snap as he switched off his mobile phone. For an instant she allowed herself to lean against the wall. There was no feeling of satisfaction in her for having been proved right. A youngster had died violently. She didn't like to think of the perky teenager being dragged into that cold vault.

'Is anything wrong, Sister?'

Hanging up the telephone she turned to Mother Dorothy. 'A young boy has been found dead, Mother. I met him once and unless some family for him can be traced I may have to go down and identify him. May I have your permission to take the van into town tomorrow morning?'

'Yes, of course. I am sorry to hear the news. You must try to set it aside during recreation.'

Recreation had never seemed more trivial. It was wrong to think that, she reminded herself. The great saint Teresa had considered laughter and enjoyment part of the holiest life. She sat with her knitting, grateful that there was no need to talk since Sister Katherine was singing folk songs to Sister Marie's guitar accompaniment.

Two people were dead. A pleasant, ordinary young girl and a tearaway lad. Both killed in the same manner but was it for the same reason? She stabbed the needle thoughtfully through the pale blue wool which was intended to turn into a sweater for her mother as a Christmas gift, and tried to fix her mind on the sweet sounds emanating from Sister Katherine.

Recreation ended having lasted in her estimation twice as long as usual, and they filed down into chapel for the final blessing of the day. She murmured the prayers of the rosary, forcing herself to concentrate on the words.

'I have no objection to your helping the police when it's absolutely necessary,' Mother Dorothy had warned her more than once, 'but you must never allow worldly matters to interfere with your spiritual life. Our first duty is to enrich our spiritual lives until they overflow and bring blessings beyond the community. A nun who only pays lip service to her vocation is spiritually impoverished and affects the whole Order.'

The day was winding down. Mother Dorothy sprinkled the holy water and the sisters filed out silently. Until morning, save in emergency, there would be silence now.

Sister Joan went through to the kitchen to begin the regular task of checking locks and bolting doors. Alice wagged her tail hopefully and stood up, obviously wanting a walk.

Sister Joan patted her, opened the back door and went out to check on Lilith. It was odd how readily animals accepted routine. During the day both Lilith and Alice displayed pique if they weren't spoken to but after the grand silence had fallen they seemed dimly to understand that for a space the time of talking was done.

It was still misty, though a slight breeze was blowing away the long strands of white that clung to the walls of the buildings and cobwebbed the dark bushes that marked the start of the shrubbery. Alice yelped suddenly and darted off through the archway.

Sister Joan hastily locked the kitchen door, stuck the key in her pocket and set off in pursuit.

The moon was struggling through the clouds to illuminate the rough path that led past the walls of the enclosure garden towards the tennis court at the other side of which stood the postulancy. Four figures, guided by Sister Hilaria's torch, were almost across the tennis court and stopped, half turning, as Alice bounded joyfully after them. There was suppressed laughter as Sister Teresa bent, grabbed Alice's collar, and threaded some string through it. Sister Teresa was the sort of person who carried in her pocket a variety of objects that could be used for almost any purpose!

She reached the little group, looped the end of the string about her wrist, and nodded her thanks as the others turned and continued their way.

Sister Joan tugged Alice to heel, privately deciding to have a serious word with her when she was free to speak again. Alice was young but she'd been bought as a guard dog and it was time she started guarding!

With that in mind she changed course and began to skirt the walls of the garden and take the path that led between high hedges of shrubbery towards the front of the house.

If she brought Alice on a tour round the convent last thing at night the silly dog might get the idea that she was supposed to patrol the property.

The mist was thinner here, the moon's rays growing brighter so that each blade of grass stood out, whole and perfect. Beyond the open gates the moor rose and fell in billows of light and shade. Someone moved from behind a thorn tree and then stood, alerted by Alice's sudden sharp bark. A tall figure, partly obscured by the shadowing branches.

Turning, the hair at the back of her head bristling, she walked back swiftly to the stableyard, her hand shaking as she turned the key in the lock, and let herself into the still warm, brightly lit kitchen. Shooting the bolt into place, drawing the blinds down, untying the makeshift lead, she silently scolded herself for arrant cowardice. The figure on the moor could've been anyone – Luther taking a late stroll or someone from the Romany camp indulging in a spot of poaching. She was going to be no help at all if she allowed her imagination to get the better of her.

The outside door leading to the chapel was unlocked as usual. She went swiftly down the corridor and across the hall. Mother Dorothy had given instructions that the outer door should be left open for any stray worshipper. On the other hand Mother Dorothy didn't know about the footprints up in the storerooms.

The chapel was deserted, the candles snuffed, the sanctuary light glowing redly. She stepped out to bolt the outer door, hoping that she was using her initiative in an approved fashion, and walked down the aisle to the Lady Altar. The iron staircase twisted up into darkness. There hadn't been time, surely, for anyone to enter the chapel. On the other hand—

She went softly up the stairs, switching on the lights as she reached the landing, holding her breath for an instant as she waited for some betraying sound. There was nothing, but she went resolutely into the storerooms, switching on more lights as she paced between the piles of boxes and broken furniture. Only her own shadow paced alongside. The upper storey was empty of intruders.

She had promised Sister David she would get a bolt fixed on the cupboard where the rarer books were kept. That had been when she'd had pocket money, she thought wryly. Now she'd have to root around in the garden shed for something suitable.

She turned off the lights and came down into the chapel again.

Going into the hall and bolting the door she had a comfortable sensation of security. They would be safe in the postulancy too, Sister Teresa being a great one for bolting and barring things.

She completed her checking of windows and doors, gave Alice a consoling stroke for having her walk cut short, and looked in at the infirmary door, to be greeted by the sound of two old ladies snoring in unison. Going up the wide staircase she was aware of an aching back. No doubt her broken sleep the previous night had taken its toll, together with the stress of the recent events. She would learn to pace herself better, she resolved.

The booklet that Sister David had found in the library lay on the shelf. Sister Joan closed her cell door, hesitated, then lit her lamp. Something about that booklet had attracted her glancing attention as she laid it down but she couldn't recall what it was. A thought, half-formed, had dissipated. Lighting one's lamp was not absolutely prohibited but it was actively discouraged. Money was too scarce for electricity to be wasted.

The booklet was an amateurish production, only the cover printed and the few sheets inside being partly printed by hand and partly typed. The cover informed the reader that they were about to look at the *Family Tree with Notes on the Tarquin Family*. The 'N' was fainter than the rest. As the half-formed thought nudged her again she scrabbled in her pocket for the crumpled circular. Yes, there was the same fainter 'N'. She must have noticed that without realizing that she had noticed it. Both the circular and the pamphlet had been printed on the same machine.

Seating herself on the floor, with her skirt tucked under her to imitate a cushion in the approved manner, she opened the pamphlet.

Her first feeling was one of disappointment. There were no grisly family secrets here for the inquisitive outsider to read, only a long list of names and dates of birth and marriage and death, with fairly long gaps where the genealogical trail had gone cold. Someone in the Tarquin family had been interested enough in the past to attempt to trace his ancestors but the tree ended abruptly, a typewritten note saying,

There is a hiatus from the beginning of the sixteenth century to the end of it. Presumably the direct descendants of Sir Richard Tarquine kept a low profile during the religious and political troubles of that century. Sir Richard himself had a most distinguished career, serving the Earl of Warwick during the Hundred Years' War, and building a manor house on his return from the campaign which would later provide the foundations of the larger house built in the early eighteenth century. I fear that more modern members of the family have not always lived up to those high ideals of chivalry.

A man disappointed in his own offspring from the sound of it. She guessed that it had been Sir Robert Tarquin who had sold his estate to the Order of Daughters of Compassion, and left his only son only sufficient to build a house and probably live modestly.

There was nothing more to justify her keeping her lamp on any longer. She turned it off and groped to the small window to adjust the blind.

Moonlight pooled the yard. She could see it whitening the cobbles. The stable was in blacker shadow with no sound from Lilith. From the kitchen Alice gave a sudden loud bark, and a figure moved from the lee of the stable and stood for a moment as if deliberating his next move.

Had the Day of Judgement been announced she couldn't have stirred in that long moment as Grant Tarquin raised his moon-whitened face, made whiter by the black hair and glinting black eyes, and looked up at her, his sensual lips parting in a smile before with infinitely chilling courtesy he bowed, then spun around and was part of the darkness again.

Nine

Driving across the moor the next morning, rain blurring the windscreen of the van, she tried not to think of that white-faced figure, standing beneath her window, some kind of black garment wrapped around him. Grant Tarquin had enjoyed a flair for the dramatic, she recalled. And it had been Grant Tarquin she had seen.

Brother Cuthbert waved and mouthed something at her as she drove past and she waved back, not stopping since the clock on the dashboard informed her it was already half past nine. When a crime had been committed time was important.

Detective Sergeant Mill was on the steps of the police station. As she pulled into the yard the thought crossed her mind that he wasn't unlike Grant Tarquin in outward aspect, but happily lacked that darkness of spirit that had laid such a corruption over the masculine beauty of the other.

'Leave the van here, Sister.' He came to the door. 'We can go to the morgue in my car.'

'Nobody's come forward then to identify him?' Changing vehicles, she glanced at him.

'Oh, there are plenty of youngsters who could identify him,' he said, getting behind the wheel, 'but I need to know if he was the lad who guarded your van when you went for petrol. That would put him in the vicinity of the office in Nightingale Court a couple of days before Jane Sinclair was killed. It's possible he saw something that might have made him a threat.'

She was silent, considering. It was possible that Jeb had seen someone hanging about and taken the extremely unwise course of trying to obtain a few pounds hush money. If he had then he couldn't have realized he was dealing with a very ruthless individual.

Morgues didn't frighten her but they did depress her. The cold, impersonal atmosphere made her spirits sink, though her common sense told her that it was foolish to allow emotion to cloud professional judgement. She compressed her lips as the sheet was drawn back, took a moment to look at the young, dead face, crossed herself and said, 'Yes, that's the boy I saw in Nightingale Court.'

'Thank you, Sister. Shall we sit in the car?'

In the cool, damp air again she drew several deep breaths before getting back into the car.

'Will you require Sister Gabrielle to identify him as the boy who broke into the chapel?' she asked.

'If it has nothing to do with his death, then there's no point in bringing her into it,' Detective Sergeant Mill said. 'I wouldn't want the good Sisters to get the reputation of being cane-wielding thugs! It was only a glancing blow according to the doctor, caused a superficial cut and a bit of a black eye. His death was due to strangulation, manual strangulation.'

'You said you know who he was – Jeb, I mean.'

'Jeb Jones, seventeen years old, brought up in a children's home, school dropout, left London about six months ago and drifted to Cornwall. No criminal record, though I daresay he wasn't too scrupulous about the ways in which he earned a few pounds. He was one of those kids who drop through the social security net. A bit of a victim.'

'Poor Jeb!' Sister Joan grimaced slightly, not liking the picture of the life he had sketched for her. 'Hadn't he friends?'

'He didn't stay long enough in any one place to form strong relationships. He's been squatting in the Tarquin house for about a month as far as we can gather. Of course the local council are supposed to check up on these places but apparently he was quiet and made no trouble so nobody bothered.'

'Grant Tarquin must've known he was there,' Sister Joan said.

There was a pause. Detective Sergeant Mill stared at her, then said brusquely, 'Would you tell me what the devil you mean?'

'Jane Sinclair telephoned me and spoke of Grant Tarquin and

resurrection,' Sister Joan said. 'She'd been looking at an album of old Tarquin photographs with Anne Dalton. I borrowed the album myself and there are photographs in it of Grant Tarquin's grandfather – there's a very strong family resemblance running through the generations. I think she saw Grant Tarquin and recognized him from the photographs. It must've worried her because she knew he was dead. She liked to walk in the old cemetery and she must've seen his grave. I think that was what she wanted to talk to me about but she was phoning from her lodgings where the telephone's kept in the hall and she may have felt awkward about saying too much with Anne Dalton around.'

'And then?'

'On the morning she was due to meet me for coffee she had a phone call,' Sister Joan reminded him. 'Anne Dalton said it was a gentleman. Now he might have told her he was a police officer and her office had been broken into so Jane Sinclair would have gone there early and he was waiting.'

'He being?'

'Last night,' she said steadily, 'I was looking through my window. It looks down into the stableyard. It was past eleven – the rest of the community were in bed but it's my job to go round and switch off lights and lock up last thing. Earlier, when I was bringing Alice in, I saw a man standing beyond the front gates. It was too misty to identify him but I got stupidly nervous and hurried indoors. Then, when I looked out of my cell window, I saw someone move out of the shadow of the stable into the yard. The moonlight was very bright and I saw him clearly when he raised his face. It was Grant Tarquin. I recognized him. He's a striking-looking man.'

'*Was* a striking-looking man. He died more than a year ago.'

'He looked up at me and then he bowed.' She shivered slightly.

'Are you absolutely certain about all this?' he demanded.

'Absolutely certain,' she said calmly. 'Grant Tarquin is still alive, Alan. I saw him last night. If you open the grave in the old cemetery it's my guess that you'll find a pile of stones.'

'My good girl, I can't go round digging up the dead!' he said impatiently. 'I'd have to obtain an exhumation order from the Home Office, and I'm afraid they wouldn't issue one on the grounds I've got.'

'You'll make enquiries into the circumstances of Grant Tarquin's death though?'

'Yes, of course. If I can find any more substantial reason for applying for an exhumation order then I'll do so immediately. Meanwhile you'll oblige me by not wandering about by yourself, particularly after dark. I already told you that!'

'You can't tell me to do anything,' Sister Joan said, stung by his tone. 'I'm not one of your officers! You can advise me and naturally I always try to follow your advice but my first obedience has to be to the rule. You know that!'

'I could always speak to Mother Dorothy.'

'Mother Dorothy is worried about our financial situation so don't give her anything else to trouble her,' she said sharply. 'Look, I will take the greatest care in future, I promise! Now can we go and do something practical instead of arguing?'

'What were you thinking of doing?'

'I'd like to return the album of photographs to Anne Dalton and have a quick look round the cemetery. Have you time? The album's in the van.'

'Right!' He leaned forward to turn the ignition key. 'Would you mind if I had a look at it myself first? I can give it back to Anne Dalton on your behalf when I go round there to meet the Sinclairs. They're arriving shortly to identify their daughter and arrange the funeral.'

'Yes, of course. Thank you.'

They reached the police station and she climbed into the van and took out the album.

'Look, if you're busy I can take a look round the old cemetery myself,' she began.

'I'll come with you,' he said firmly. 'We'll use my car. I don't trust my life and limb in that monstrosity you drive.'

'It's better than the old car we used to have,' she protested. 'Brother Cuthbert loves tinkering with that old engine, but I doubt if he'll ever get it to go.'

The irritation between them had gone. It wasn't anybody's fault, she reasoned, as they turned into Cemetery Road. He thought like a policeman and had little sympathy with the different rules by which she had to organize her life.

'I take it the place has been searched?' She glanced

enquiringly at him as they entered the cemetery.

'It's still being searched.' He nodded towards two policemen who were walking, slow and stooped, across the overgrown paths. 'Unfortunately it's rained fairly heavily again since last night but if the person who brought Jeb here left any traces we'll find them.'

'How was he brought here?' she asked.

'My guess is that the killer was already in the house when you arrived. You said you didn't search any of the rooms thoroughly – in any case the house has a cellar, so he might've nipped down there. Then, as soon as you left, he went upstairs, wrapped the body in a rug and walked to the old cemetery.'

'Have you found the rug?'

'That's only my theory. It'll have been a rug or a thick blanket, something a strong man could carry over his shoulder without attracting too much attention. Also it was a damp, misty Sunday afternoon. There weren't many people around. If he was seen then someone will come forward. There are house-to-house enquiries going on.'

'And Jeb was in the old chapel? May we go there?'

'It's off limits to members of the public,' he reminded her, 'but you're not exactly an idle sightseer. Come on.'

There was a policeman on duty outside the low stone edifice. Sister Joan, going past him with Detective Sergeant Mill at her heels, reflected that some extra men must have been drafted in from other stations. Inside the stone walls seemed to press in around her and she repressed a shudder.

'You all right?' He glanced at her as they went up the aisle.

'Fine. Can we turn on those lamps?' She pointed to an array of them clearly set up by the investigating team.

'If you like.'

He crossed to switch them on and the gloom was banished by a white glare. There was nothing mellow about this light, she thought, blinking. It was a cold, pitiless light that searched out the truth.

'There were no footprints?'

'Long scraping marks. It's my belief that when he'd dumped the body – over there between the two tombs – he dragged the rug or whatever it was over any footprints he'd left. When we find the rug we'll have more to go on.'

Nothing appeared to have been altered since her previous visit. She bit her lip as she looked at the jumble of broken chairs, the two tombs with their recumbent figures.

'Both Tarquins,' Detective Sergeant Mill said. 'The older one seems to have been quite a distinguished fellow. Fought in the Hundred Years' War.'

'And served the Earl of Warwick who bought Jeanne d'Arc from the Burgundians,' Sister Joan said disapprovingly. 'It was Warwick and his men who insisted on the death sentence being carried out. I'd not want to be ennobled by such a man!'

'Surely he was only acting on behalf of the English Council.'

'He probably enjoyed it,' she said testily. 'To tell you the truth apart from a few honourable exceptions I don't think the Tarquins were very pleasant people.'

'But very rich.'

'There are advantages in poverty.'

'One wouldn't think so the way you and your sisters are always fretting about money,' he observed.

'Poverty doesn't have to mean starving to death. We take a vow of poverty, which means that we share anything we earn for the welfare of the community. If we can't earn our bread we don't trot down and sign on at the local labour exchange. But we're lucky all the same. At least we have a roof over our heads and a garden where we can grow food, and no need to wheel and deal and squat in empty houses. Thank you for letting me come in here.'

'What were you hoping to find?' he asked.

'I haven't the faintest idea,' she said. 'I suppose I had some stupid notion that I'd spot something you missed, but of course I didn't. Sorry if I've wasted your time.'

'You haven't.' He stood aside to let her go through the door. 'Your ideas are never dull, Sister, and sometimes you manage to hit the nail on the head. Oh, I do have a piece of information for you. There was a small printing press down in the cellar at the Tarquin house. The N is faint on it. Looks as if the press came originally from the estate. Perhaps Grant Tarquin had some notion of setting up a small business.'

'In scrap metal and silverware?' She raised a disbelieving eyebrow. 'He probably had some notion of sending anonymous letters or distributing pornography.'

'Now you're speaking ill of the dead.'

'He's not dead!' she said. 'I saw him last night. He was alive then.'

'Sister, if the family was as immoral as you say there might be descendants on the wrong side of the blanket all over Cornwall,' he said patiently.

'I'd already considered that,' she retorted. 'It won't do, Alan. There's a difference between seeing someone who bears a strong resemblance to somebody else and seeing the actual person.'

'You only met Grant Tarquin a couple of times.'

'It was enough,' she said tensely. 'There was an – an aura about him – something to be felt rather than seen, something extremely beguiling and evil.'

'You're not going mystical on me, are you?' His smile was slightly down-curving.

'No, of course not! I'm trying to explain my instinct about all this. You use your own instinct, don't you? Otherwise why do you keep referring to the killer as *him*, when you don't know whether it is.'

'Strangling isn't usually a woman's method,' he said. 'Especially manual strangulation. It requires terrific strength in the thumbs and wrists. Also, whoever moved Jeb's body must have beeen pretty strong. I may be wrong, and a six-foot female who practises weightlifting will turn up, but I don't think so. Yes?'

He turned from her abruptly as one of the two men they had seen searching the paths came up.

'We've found something, sir,' the policeman said. 'You might like to take a look.'

'Come along, Sister.' He motioned the policeman ahead of them down the path as it curved away from the grass verge.

The other man was standing by the grave of Grant Tarquin, his eyes on the pile of wet brushwood that covered its weed-encrusted surface.

'There's something under there,' he said.

'Let's take a look.' Detective Sergeant Mill went down on one knee and gently lifted a few pieces of the brushwood.

The corner of a grimy blanket protruded.

'We'd better get the photographer back before we move it,'

Detective Sergeant Mill said, rising, dusting the knee of his trouser leg. 'Sister Joan, was all this brushwood here when you visited the grave?'

'No,' Sister Joan said.

'Right, we'd better get on with things. I'll run you back to the station so you can pick up the van. Back in ten minutes.'

He nodded to the guarding men and hurried Sister Joan to the opening in the wall.

'You're needed here,' she said. 'It's only a short walk to the station. I could've gone by myself to the cemetery too, it was already crawling with police!'

'Perhaps I enjoy your company,' he said.

'In that case I'll certainly walk back alone!' she said, with a flash of laughter.

'If you're sure?'

'Quite sure.'

She was walking away when he called after her, 'One more thing, Sister!'

'Yes?'

'I intend to make some enquiries about Grant Tarquin's death,' he said.

'Thank you.' She smiled and walked swiftly down the road.

Cutting up the alley she passed the Tarquin house. A small gaggle of reporters was hanging round the broken gates, and two policemen now stood on guard. The slowly emerging sunlight was mocked by the dense coat of ivy infesting the walls and the tall, mist-soaked grass in the neglected garden.

For once she would be in time for lunch, she thought, as she drove back along the main street and turned off on to the moorland track. She would finish the organization of the various excerpts from the books about Jeanne d'Arc and later on get back to clearing the storerooms. The work there was going slowly. Perhaps the boy Jeb had been paid to break in and steal the photograph with its sinister boast. No, the photograph had been of Grant Tarquin's grandfather or even great grandfather. He'd never been so sensitive about the reputation of his family. Who would care if someone long dead had amused himself with a little devil worship?

Brother Cuthbert was bent over the old car, head buried in its innards as she drove by. Odd that a young man who had embraced an ascetic medieval discipline should be so crazy about a heap of rusting machinery – almost as odd, she thought with a grin as a nun who got involved with murder.

The convent presented its usual air of quiet, well-organized activity. Sister Teresa was peeling potatoes, Sister Marie mucking out the stable while Alice yapped with delight round her ankles. In the main hall Sister David met her, a pile of letters in her hand.

'I typed out the excerpts you marked and put them on the desk in the library in chronological order,' she said. 'You only have the linking bits to write now.'

'Thank you very much, Sister – and I haven't forgotten about putting a bolt on the cupboard,' Sister Joan said.

'I'm rather looking forward to the readings this week,' Sister David said. 'It would be nice if we each of us researched our patron saints and read their stories when our turn in the rota came round, don't you think? Perhaps I'll suggest it to Mother Dorothy.'

'Nothing to do except chatter, Sister David?' Mother Dorothy had emerged from the antechamber. 'It isn't like you to – ah! you're with Sister Joan. That explains it!'

'We were discussing the suppertime readings, Mother Prioress,' Sister David hastened to explain. 'I began the conversation.'

'If you've finished the letters you'd better put them on the hall table,' Mother Dorothy instructed. 'Sister Joan will post them the next time she has to drive into town. Have you a moment, Sister?'

'Yes, Mother Prioress.'

Following her superior she wondered if the day would ever dawn when Mother Dorothy informed her she was an exemplary nun, a shining credit to the Order.

'*Dominus vobiscum.*' Mother Dorothy signalled her to close the parlour door.

'*Et cum spiritu tuo.*'

'Sit down, Sister. Did your errand in town go well?'

'It was productive, Mother Dorothy,' Sister Joan said cautiously.

'Padraic Lee came by this morning, full of gossip as usual,' Mother Dorothy said. 'A young woman strangled and now a teenage boy. I assume you're mixed up in it all.'

'Only indirectly,' Sister Joan said. 'I met Jane Sinclair the one time and I met the boy Jeb Jones when the petrol was siphoned out of the van.'

'You must, of course, give whatever help you can in these civil matters,' Mother Dorothy said, 'but I must warn you again not to neglect your spiritual duties. I am sure you never mean to but balancing the mundane and the spiritual is always a great struggle. At the moment I know only too well how difficult it is. I seem to spend all my time wrestling with the bills and trying to make economies when I yearn to concentrate on making this convent a channel of prayer. So I'm not unsympathetic to your situation. Now you'd better get on with your work, Sister. I hope you are going to give us Jeanne the woman and not Jeanne the icon from the history books. It is far more of an encouragement to us all if we can realize that even the greatest saints were fallible human beings. *Dominus vobiscum.'*

'Thank you, Mother Prioress. *Dominus vobiscum.'*

Sister Joan knelt, rose and went out, glancing back at the door to see her superior already turning the pages of a threatening-looking red ledger.

Sister David's neatly typed notes were ranged on the library desk. She sat down and began to read through them carefully, making the linking notes as she went along.

She had kept the history of the various battles to a minimum and scarcely mentioned the various miracles attributed to the French saint. They might have been absolutely genuine but it had all been a very long time ago, before science could have provided any explanation. Uneasily aware that her thoughts were tending in a decidedly heretical direction, she crossed out the word 'telepathy' and penned in the word 'visionary' instead. No sense in upsetting the more traditionally minded among the community!

At least she had made her subject sound like a living, breathing human being, not one of those pious waxwork figures one couldn't feel any sympathy with. Her Jeanne was a tough, illiterate, humorous, highly intelligent young peasant with a sharp tongue and a limitless fund of compassion. She would certainly have cared about the deaths of Jane Sinclair and Jeb Jones. She had wept when her page was killed by a stray arrow, wept when her two rings and her sword were stolen from her, wept when it was time to face the fire.

'Sister Joan?'

She jumped violently, her hand to her mouth, as a figure loomed in the doorway.

'I'm sorry, child. I didn't mean to frighen you,' Sister Gabrielle said. 'I thought that the tapping of my stick could be heard half a mile off.'

'I was deep in thought, Sister. I'm sorry. You should've called out so I could've helped you up the stairs.'

'I'm nearly eighty-seven, not nearly a hundred and eighty-seven,' Sister Gabrielle said in her peppery way. 'I'm still capable of climbing a few steps. Sister, ought I to go to the police? Mother Dorothy, as you know, gets a newspaper once a week, and she often tells me little pieces of news she doesn't tell the rest, and a young boy has been killed. I couldn't help wondering – in view of the fact that you've begun popping down into town constantly – would it be the same lad who – my conscience is bothering me.'

'It was the same lad,' Sister Joan said frankly, 'but your hitting him on the nose had nothing to do with anything that happened to him later. I told Detective Sergeant Mill about the incident and he said there was no need for you to be brought into it at all.'

'Well, you've relieved my mind a little,' Sister Gabrielle said. 'Do they know who killed him yet?'

Sister Joan shook her head.

'Well, I shall pray for his soul.' The old lady nodded once or twice, then tapped her way across the room. 'It's a long time since I've been up here. Mary Concepta will be jealous when I let her know. We seem to have acquired a lot of new books. Of course we were in possession of quite a considerable little library when we moved here but there are many more volumes now. Love stories and sex manuals I wouldn't be surprised! The rules aren't as strict as they used to be.'

'They seem quite strict enough to me,' Sister Joan said, amused.

'You young ones don't know you're born,' Sister Gabrielle said. 'Well, why should you? We've abolished evil and put social problems in its place.'

'You must've been in the Order when a convent was founded here,' Sister Joan said.

'Of course I was. We had a house further north but it was small and in very bad repair and we were looking round for something bigger and more convenient. I remember old Sir Robert Tarquin coming to offer us this estate at a very reasonable price. Actually he wasn't so old, early fifties, I think, but he had a certain presence and great dignity. He seemed careworn, disappointed in his son, I daresay. Grant Tarquin wasn't a very nice person, my dear.'

'Do you think he could've been a devil worshipper?' Sister Joan asked bluntly.

'A devil—! My dear child, what put that into your head?' Sister Gabrielle stared at her. 'No, of course not. Mind you, there was a rumour that Sir Robert's father had been rather more familiar with Old Nick than was healthy. I fancy he used to enjoy terrifying the servants with mysterious hints – that kind of thing. No, real devil worshippers are thin on the ground, thank God! Some of these old families were a bit inbred, I expect. Not quite one hundred percent in the head. Are you coming down to lunch?'

'Very soon, Sister, unless you'd like me to—'

'I can get down steps a lot more easily than I can climb up 'em,' Sister Gabrielle assured her. 'I'm glad my blow didn't do much damage, though I was only defending myself. We're to have Jeanne d'Arc at supper then?'

'Yes.'

'I hope you're not going to dwell on all that burning business,' the old lady said briskly. 'It does put one off one's food. I won't forget Sister Perpetua reading about some saint who had his insides dragged out of him. We were having spaghetti with tomato sauce at the time, and I've not felt the same about it since.'

Sister Joan choked back laughter and said, 'No details of the burning I promise. Oh, Sister David was suggesting earlier that it might be a nice idea if each of us concentrated on her patron as her turn came round to read. St Gabriel would be an interesting subject.'

'The Archangel.' Sister Gabrielle looked doubtful. 'Well, he didn't die a stomach-churning death but then he was never actually born, was he? To tell you the truth, my dear, I've never been particularly struck on the Archangel Gabriel. Always flying around giving people messages and blowing that trumpet of his! And when I found out he's the archangel of water – well, I can't help it, but every time I try to picture him I see him wringing out his wings with wellington boots on his feet.'

It was no good trying to concentrate on the last few notes after that. Sister Joan shook with silent mirth as the old lady tapped her way back down into the chapel, then wiped her eyes and rose.

So Mother Dorothy had read about Jeb's murder in the weekly newspaper from which she read out any items of interest to the rest of the community. Her own attempt to protect her from any additional worries had failed. At least Mother Dorothy was now aware that she had a legitimate reason to help Detective Sergeant Mill. What she had to ensure, though it would be hard, was that helping the police didn't interfere more than was necessary with her life in the community.

She paused on the landing and then stepped aside into the long storerooms, the smile fading on her lips as she surveyed the long gloomy aisles. She had cleared a lot of rubbish and given the broken kitchen chairs to Sister Martha who would find a use for them in the garden somewhere, and the piles of old newspapers were stacked now in the wardrobe but there were dozens of boxes and bales and old chests and wicker baskets stuffed to overflowing with dirty, cracked crockery.

Sir Robert Tarquin might've been a generous man but it was highly unlikely that he'd left anything of value in the house when he sold it to the Daughters of Compassion. There would be no cache of precious stones, no long-forgotten Old Master, nothing but rubbish.

And if there is anything, she thought impatiently, then I wish St Gabriel would empty the water out of his wellington boots and give me a hint.

Downstairs the bell sounded for lunch. In the far corner of the storerooms a board groaned and settled dustily. Sister Joan sighed and went slowly down the stairs.

Ten

Monday had passed quietly. Sister Joan, drinking her cup of breakfast coffee on Tuesday, hoped it wasn't the calm before the storm. She had made excellent headway the previous afternoon in clearing the storerooms, managing to clear out half a dozen orange boxes filled with broken crockery and rusted cutlery – hadn't the Tarquins ever thrown anything away? A flat, leather-covered case at the bottom of the last box had yielded a handsome necklace set with amber which she'd carried down in triumph to Mother Dorothy.

'The silver isn't first-rate quality but the amber is pretty,' the prioress had said, peering at the necklace. 'A gold setting would triple the value. However once it's cleaned up it might fetch a hundred and fifty. You've done well, Sister.'

'There are half a dozen spoons too, Mother Dorothy. They're silver, I think.' The spoons had been duly examined and Mother Dorothy had lifted her head, her face positively benign.

'These are Hester Bateman spoons,' she'd pronounced. 'They'll bring in a good price, about a hundred each probably. Excellent!'

'I didn't realize you were an expert, Mother,' Sister Joan said.

'Hardly that.' Mother Dorothy shook her head. 'My father was a jeweller who dabbled in antiques, and I picked up some useful scraps of knowledge when I was a girl. Now we'll get these cleaned and I'll make some enquiries about current market value.'

She nodded pleasantly, leaving Sister Joan to ponder on the fact that this was the first time her superior had ever mentioned her life in the world before she entered the Order. Usually she behaved as if she'd been born with a veil on her head. She also actively discouraged the others from mentioning the lives they had led in the world, since detachment had to be practised assiduously. Sister Joan wondered if Mother Dorothy was mellowing. A few moments later, hearing her scolding Sister Marie for slopping some water, she decided that she wasn't.

'We enjoyed your reading last night,' Sister Katherine said, approaching. 'I've always loved the story of Jeanne d'Arc.'

'And her favourite saint was Saint Katherine,' Sister Joan said.

'I know. Some people say that Saint Katherine never existed, but I find that very hard to believe. What do you think?'

'I think that because there isn't scientific proof for anything that doesn't mean that it doesn't exist,' Sister Joan said.

'Excuse me, Sister,' Mother Dorothy broke in. 'There was a telephone call earlier for you from Detective Sergeant Mill. Jane Sinclair is to be laid to rest this afternoon in the new municipal cemetery and he wondered if we wished to send a representative. Miss Sinclair wasn't a Catholic but as you actually met her and as she had made very few friends in the district I thought it would be a nice gesture if you were to go. They are sending a car for you after lunch. Sister Martha will make up a posy of whatever flowers are still available. You will join the funeral party at the graveside but not, of course, attend the Protestant service.'

'Yes, Mother Prioress.'

Whatever His Holiness in Rome said, Mother Dorothy had grave reservations about the ecumenical movement.

She filled the morning with housework, it being her turn to assist Sister Teresa which was convenient since Sister Marie was scrubbing the stonework as a penance for her earlier carelessness. Sister Joan shot her a sympathetic look as she collected polishing cloths and the cake of beeswax with which the wooden floors were still burnished to perfection, but the round-faced novice looked quite cheerful despite the damp air that would make her task unpleasant. She would make a good nun when she had made her final profession.

Polishing gave one time in which to think. Sister Joan proceeded to think about recent events, to place them in some kind of order in her mind. The decision had been made to clear out the storerooms and she had mentioned it to Luther who had gone off and chattered about it. Someone – Mr Monam? –

had heard and hastily printed the circular and registered with the Falcon Agency. No, there was something wrong there. It had happened too quickly. Mr Monam must have already been registered with the telephone answering service before he'd heard Luther's chatter. The circular must have been printed already and thrust through the convent door as soon as he learned the clearance of the storerooms was imminent. It didn't make sense, she decided. Rather, it must make sense but a piece of the pattern was still missing. She went on thinking, recalling her own visit to Nightingale Court, her brief meetings with Jane Sinclair and young Jeb Jones. And then Jane Sinclair, who liked walking in the old cemetery and looking at Victorian photograph albums, had rung to arrange a meeting with her, a meeting she had never kept because a phone call had taken her to the office where her killer was waiting. Why had she been killed at that particular time? Who had known she had information she wanted to pass on? There was another bit of the pattern missing there too.

'If you polish that bit one more time,' Sister Perpetua observed, coming through the hall with a basket of washing, 'we'll all break our necks and you'll be responsible, Sister. Do move on to another part! It'll be lunchtime soon.'

'Sorry, Sister!' She hastily shuffled along and resumed her work, pushing the broken bits of pattern to the back of her mind.

Detective Sergeant Mill was driving the squad car when she went out to meet it after lunch. He had put on a dark suit and a black tie, and gave the posy of late heather and ferns she was carrying a glance of appreciation as she got in the car.

'A nice gesture, Sister. I'm glad you got permission to come. There won't be many there, I'm afraid, though we can expect quite a few reporters.'

'Did you meet her parents?' she asked.

'A nice ordinary couple. They're bearing up very well. Mrs Dalton will be there and the Falcon Agency are sending a representative, but that's about it. Jane Sinclair didn't make much impact on the world.'

'Sufficient to get herself killed,' she reproved.

'That's true.'

She shivered slightly. 'Alan, I've been trying to put things in order and they won't go. I told Luther we were going to clear out the storerooms and within twenty-four hours someone printed a circular and put it through our front door and got an estimate sheet into the filing cabinet in Nightingale Court, having already registered with the Falcon Agency – there wasn't time.'

'Perhaps the two murders had nothing to do with the fact that you're starting a spot of spring cleaning,' he said slowly.

'But it has something to do with the Tarquins!' she explained. 'The boy was killed in the empty house that Grant Tarquin built for himself and then carried to the old chapel with the two Tarquin tombs in it, and the blanket – do you know anything about the blanket yet?'

'It's still being examined. If there's a single hair from Jeb Jones's head, or a few drops of sweat then we can tie it in scientifically.'

'Never mind scientific – what do you think?' she demanded.

'I think it's the blanket used to wrap up Jeb's body and carry him over to the old cemetery.'

'And then laid on Grant Tarquin's grave and covered with all that brushwood.'

'Again pointing to the Tarquins – which seems careless if it was a member of the family who committed the murders.'

'Not careless, deliberate,' Sister Joan said. 'Someone who likes taking risks and feels quite sure he'll get away with it. Someone mocking us all the way. Alan, you may scoff as much as you like but I'm positive that Grant Tarquin stood beneath my window the other night. I do wish—'

'I've made some enquiries,' he said, swinging the car neatly to the right and driving down the high street past the small railway station and on to the dual carriageway.

'And?'

'Grant Tarquin left the district and went abroad just after you came to Cornwall,' he said.

'Yes, I know that.'*

'He went to the Middle East – Turkey, Cyprus then Algeria – travelling light. He must've returned to this country once or twice, since one or two people saw him but he never stayed for more than a day or two and, as he was perfectly entitled to

* See *Vow of Silence*

come and check on his house, nobody took much notice. He died out in Turkey – a road accident. A Dr Gullegein signed the death certificate and made arrangements for the body to be flown back to England and buried. He'd left money with his solicitors to cover that.'

'Psychic, was he?'

'It's perfectly normal for someone to make provision for the unexpected if they spend most of their time abroad but wish to be buried in their native land. Anyway he'd already purchased a burial plot for himself and everything was very quietly arranged.'

'So the body was flown home and quietly buried. Did anyone identify it?'

'The doctor who signed the death certificate was well acquainted with Grant Tarquin. Sister, Turkey is on the fringes of Europe. They have television there and fast food.'

'Have you contacted this Dr Gullegein?'

'I rang our consul there. Dr Gullegein left the country about eighteen months ago and went to do voluntary work in Sudan.'

'Do you know anyone very high up in the Home Office?'

'If I did I wouldn't be a detective sergeant in the wilds of Cornwall,' he said with a grin.

'Isn't there a case for exhuming the body of Grant Tarquin because the blanket was hidden on his grave? Alan, I wouldn't ask but my instincts tell me that you'll only find bricks in that coffin.'

'Here's the new municipal cemetery.' He slowed down as he turned in the gates.

'Alan?'

'I know a couple of fellows who might agree to grant the exhumation order,' he said reluctantly, 'and the High Sheriff might go along with a request from me, but it's by no means certain.'

'But you'll try?' Her glance was eager.

'Lord help the man who tries to avoid your requests!' he said. 'Yes, Sister, I'll try. Come on. We'll park here and walk the last hundred yards.'

There was a small knot of people gathered round the graveside. A youngish woman in a black coat and hat leaned on the arm of a tall, balding man with a black band round his sleeve. There was a smartly dressed young woman in a grey suit with a brooch representing a falcon on her lapel, two or three inquisitive looking spectators, a couple of photographers and, standing a little apart with a scarf over her head and a bunch of flowers clutched in her hand, Anne Dalton. The ceremony was half over. Sister Joan moved to stand next to Anne Dalton who gave her a somewhat watery smile before she returned her attention to the ceremony again.

Was the murderer here too? There was some reason for supposing that the old belief that murderers felt compelled to attend the funerals of their victims was true, Alan Hill had told her once. Hiding nearby? She looked round and decided that was impossible. The new cemetery had none of the melancholy charm of the Victorian one. There were no weeds here, no paths twisting between high granite and marble monuments. The deceased were laid out in straight rows like patients tucked up by an old-fashioned matron and forbidden to move until Doctor had done his rounds. The headstones were uniform, upright lozenges.

'That was very sad,' Anne Dalton whispered, dabbing her eyes as she stepped back from the edge where she had placed her flowers. 'Such a nice little family. They did think of taking her home, you know, but the expense and the trauma would be too much Mr Sinclair decided, and naturally I promised to keep the grave tidy and look in from time to time.'

'I'd like a word in a moment if I may,' Sister Joan whispered back, and stepped to lay her own modest posy before she stepped over to the Sinclairs who were talking to Detective Sergeant Mill.

'Sister Joan, come and meet Mr and Mrs Sinclair,' he invited, turning. 'As I was saying Sister Joan met your daughter.'

'I had business connected with the firm she worked for,' Sister Joan said, shaking hands. 'She was very friendly and helpful. I'm truly sorry about what happened.'

'We brought her up to be friendly and obliging,' Mr Sinclair said. He sounded bewildered as if in his world friendly, obliging girls didn't get killed.

'She wanted a bit of independence,' Mrs Sinclair said. 'Wanted to try her wings. We encouraged her, didn't we, John? Maybe if we hadn't—'

'Now we can't go blaming ourselves,' her husband said. 'We can't, Melly.'

'Dreadful things happen everywhere,' Sister Joan said. 'You have my condolences.' Which would be useless if the man who had strangled Jane Sinclair wasn't brought to justice, she thought, turning away, conscious that her presence here had scarcely been registered by the grieving parents.

'It was very good of you to come, Sister,' Anne Dalton said as Sister Joan rejoined her and they began to walk slowly along the path together. 'I'm sure they appreciated it. And now a boy's been killed too, hasn't he? It makes me very nervous.'

'I was wondering about the phone call that Jane Sinclair received on the morning of her death,' Sister Joan said.

'I didn't recognize the voice,' Anne Dalton said. 'I told the police that. It wasn't anybody I knew. I couldn't identify it at all.'

'You've probably been asked this already,' Sister Joan said, 'but I did wonder if she'd seemed worried before she got the phone call. A couple of days before, perhaps? After she'd looked at the photograph album?'

'Not that I can recall. Oh, thank you for returning it by the way. No, we were just having a cup of tea late on as I told you and then she took it upstairs to have a longer look at it. I was telling her about the Tarquin family. She wanted to know if any of them were left. I told her not one. Funny that, isn't it? That family was a handsome one judging from the photographs and now they're all gone and Jane Sinclair too.'

They were not all gone, Sister Joan thought fiercely. At some point Jane Sinclair had seen somebody, perhaps fleetingly while she strolled in the old cemetery, and recognized the likeness in the old album, and having ascertained that all the Tarquins had died out, had telephoned to arrange a meeting.

'Mrs Dalton, can we give you a lift home?' Detective Sergeant Mill had joined them.

'That's very kind.' Anne Dalton was the sort of woman who blushed when an attractive man spoke to her. 'Mr and Mrs Sinclair offered but I thought it proper to leave them their privacy. Miss Clare from the Falcon Agency brought her own car and very kindly offered me transport.'

'Come along, Sister.' Detective Sergeant Mill coughed hintingly.

'You don't think—' Sister Joan shook hands with Anne Dalton and fell obediently into step.

'What don't I think?'

'That Anne Dalton might be in danger? If she knows something without knowing that she knows it—?'

'She gave a very full statement to us,' he said, 'but just for your peace of mind, Sister, we are keeping a close protective eye on her.'

'Thank you.' She sent him a grateful glance.

'How's the clearing out going on?' he asked.

'Slowly but surely. I haven't come across anything that anybody would want to steal yet. There's a very pretty amber necklace and some Hester Bateman spoons, and they'll fetch something but that's all so far.'

'Jeb could have been sneaking into the chapel in the hope of nicking something from the altar.'

'Oh, surely not!'

'Murder victims aren't all saints, Sister. He probably siphoned off your petrol anyway.'

'That's different. Have you picked up any prints from the Tarquin house except those of Jeb Jones?'

'They're still going through the place with a fine-tooth comb,' he said. 'So far nothing.'

It wasn't satisfactory but she held her peace. When he dropped her at the convent she managed to avoid asking him again to apply for an exhumation, and was rewarded by a cordial, 'I'll get on to the Sheriff as soon as I get back to the station, Sister, but don't hold your breath while we're waiting for an exhumation order. Take care of yourself now.'

'You too. God bless.' She lifted her hand in a gesture of farewell and went briskly up the shallow steps. It still wanted an hour to the afternoon cup of tea and the talk or discussion group which generally followed it. Time to do some more clearing out, she decided.

'Sister Joan, did the funeral go well?'

Mother Dorothy emerged from the anteroom.

'Yes, Mother Prioress. There weren't very many people there so Mr and Mrs Sinclair appreciated your sending me.'

'You'd better get back to the clearing out,' Mother Dorothy advised. 'Oh, if you wish you are excused from the discussion group this afternoon. We are going to debate the rights and wrongs of individuality in the religious life – hardly a subject on which you require much enlightenment.'

'No, Mother,' Sister Joan said, somewhat heartened by the twinkle behind the steel-framed spectacles.

In the chapel she knelt briefly to pray for the souls of Jane Sinclair and Jeb Jones, and then went up to the library. Sister David was on her way down, pausing to ask anxiously, 'I hate to trouble you, Sister, but you did mention finding a lock for the cupboard.'

'I hadn't forgotten, Sister. I'll see to it as soon as I can.'

'Thank you, Sister.'

Sister David went down the stairs with her little scuttling step which made her look more like a rabbit than ever.

The storerooms were dim even on the brightest day. This afternoon they were less gloomy than usual, probably because she'd shifted some of the boxes away from where they obscured the light. The spaces between were wider now and once she had pushed up the sashes of those windows she could reach the air seemed to be marginally fresher.

She started on the smaller boxes, salvaging a rather nice cream jug which might be late Victorian and a lamp which was possibly Tiffany though its shade was stained and ragged. One tin box held a variety of small, rusted tools and a couple of old curtain rings together with what looked like a sound bolt and padlock. That would please Sister David. She took the tin downstairs and put it in the shed next to the stable. As soon as time permitted she'd clean off the rust and make the books that Sister David prized so greatly a secure home.

'You didn't have your tea, Sister.' Sister Perpetua had come into the kitchen.

'I forgot it,' Sister Joan said.

'Wash your hands and I'll pour you one now,' Sister Perpetua said. 'Yes, I know you're still clearing out the storerooms but you can't miss your cup of tea. So drink it down without argument. I've got to get Sister Gabrielle and Sister Mary Concepta to the discussion group. Mary Concepta will doze off gently and Gabrielle will hog the conversation, insisting that individuality isn't approved in any nun under the age of seventy-five! Bless their hearts!'

She pressed the scalding mug of tea into Sister Joan's hands and went out.

But we are all quite distinct and definite individuals here, Sister Joan thought, gulping down the tea and returning to the storerooms. Sister Perpetua would be a force to be reckoned with anywhere, and even Sister Katherine who's so quiet and never tries to put herself forward, has her own unique brand of sweetness. Yet we wear the same habit, follow the same rule – just like policemen save that some of them wear plain clothes, but they're all separate personalities too from Constable Petrie who hadn't yet recovered from his astonishment at finding himself married to the girl of his dreams to Alan Mill. And I'm not up here to let my mind stray! I'm supposed to be looking for something that will sell and keep the wolf from the convent door.

She disentangled a chain which might be silver from a jumble of toothpicks and nails, set it aside with the Tiffany lamp and the cream jug, pulled some cardboard boxes crammed with the insides of old toilet rolls off the top of a long wooden chest that stood against the wall and sat back on her heels.

The chest was of good, well-seasoned oak and, as far as she could see without looking at the other side, had repelled woodworm. It was plainly made with oak leaves carved in relief round the sides. Jacobean? Unfortunately it seemed to be locked. She stooped to search for the keyhole but there didn't seem to be one.

'Now if I was a burglar I'd have a jemmy in my pocket,' she muttered, leaning her hand against the carved leaves on its side as she straightened up.

There was a sharp click and the lid sprang open an inch. Not Jacobean then but one of the puzzle pieces of furniture the Victorians had loved. Stepping to it she lifted the lid and smelt the sweet sickly perfume of mildewed cloth.

'Yuk!' She pulled out a couple of blankets, holding them at arms' length, and dropped them in a cleared space on the floor.

Some part of her hoped for brocade and delicate lace, for plushy velvet and embroidered silk from India, brought back by one of the earlier Tarquins. Blankets that were definitely twentieth century and more than a little odorous were a grave disappointment.

The last blanket tugged free and she pulled off the pink sheet folded beneath it. There were no more blankets in the long chest, only the young girl who lay, her thin frame covered by a shortie nightdress with a pattern of rosebuds on the collar, her eyes closed and her face still swollen so that the marks of strangulation about her young throat were obliterated by more than time.

Eleven

'This is most distressing.' Mother Dorothy's face was drawn tight with dismay and her back was ramrod straight as if she held her emotions in check with difficulty.

'We'll try to cause you as little inconvenience as possible,' Detective Sergeant Mill said.

'I wasn't thinking of our inconvenience.' There was a faint shade of reproof in her tone. 'I was thinking of that poor girl in the trunk. Who was she and how did her body get there? Who could possibly have done such a terrible thing?'

'All questions to which we hope to get answers very shortly,' he said. 'Mother Prioress, I will be leaving a man up in the storeroom area overnight. The forensic team will be here first thing in the morning. There's no way they can reach the upper storey without going through the church?'

'I'm afraid not. We finish our morning devotions and mass by eight o'clock. After that your men must do whatever is necessary. They will, I'm sure, respect the fact that they will be coming and going on consecrated ground?'

'Anyone who doesn't will soon be reminded,' he said grimly.

'And what remains in the storerooms?'

'Will be sifted with a fine-tooth comb. Anything that isn't relevant to the investigation will be returned to you. Would you like us to sort out the rubbish from what may be of value? It would save Sister Joan a lengthy task.'

He sent her a smiling glance which Mother Dorothy intercepted with a sharp, 'Sister Joan is hardly overburdened with activities, Detective Sergeant Mill. However your offer was kindly meant and is gratefully accepted.'

'If you can let me know exactly when you're all in chapel

we'll try to work round it as far as possible,' he said, bringing out his notebook.

'Sister Joan rises at four-thirty to rouse the community at five,' the prioress said. 'We are in chapel from five-thirty until eight when we have breakfast and clean our cells. After that we are engaged in our various tasks until four, with an interval of one hour for lunch and exercise. At four we have a cup of tea followed by a debate or talk here in the parlour. At five we return to our tasks until six when we go into chapel again for an hour. Supper is at seven and is followed by recreation until nine-thirty. Then we go into chapel for the final prayers and blessings of the day. Grand silence begins at ten. Naturally the sisters often visit the chapel during the day when they have a few spare moments to renew their spiritual life.'

'It sounds a punishing routine to me,' Detective Sergeant Mill said frankly, snapping his notebook shut.

'We are all strongly motivated,' Mother Dorothy said with a gleam of humour.

'Even so!' He rose from the chair. 'All that without overtime! You have my sincere admiration, Mother Prioress!'

'We're so devoted to our boss,' Sister Joan couldn't help remarking, 'that we don't mind working for nothing!'

'Sister, really!' Mother Dorothy was smiling. 'Detective Sergeant Mill, any help we can give you we'll do so gladly. I have, of course, informed my community of what has transpired and asked them to think very carefully to see if any of them can shed any light on this affair, but I doubt if they can. That chest, I imagine, has been there for many years.'

'At least twenty and probably more according to preliminary findings,' he said.

'Then by now surely—?'

'Three stranglings, all connected with the Tarquin family, would be an amazing series of coincidences,' he said. 'We must work out what connection if any binds them.'

'Yes, of course. Detective Sergeant, is there any way of keeping the media out of this?'

'I'll give instructions they're to be discouraged, but these are fairly extensive grounds and I can't muster sufficient men to throw a cordon round the place. I can leave a couple of men to patrol – and I'm afraid the chapel area will be off limits to the public until we've finished.'

'Thank you. I shall, of course, instruct the sisters not to speak to the media, and to stay as close to the main house and the postulancy as possible at all times. Will you require any further assistance from Sister Joan?'

'It's more than likely.'

'Very well. If there's nothing more—?'

'Not this evening. Thank you, Mother Prioress.'

'Sister Joan, show Detective Sergeant Mill out,' Mother Dorothy said.

'*Dominus vobiscum.*' Sister Joan bent her knee and went out ahead of him.

'The Lord be with you,' he echoed quizzically when they were in the hall. 'Does that phrase have any meaning for you all but – no, it can't have? It's automatic as ''How are you?'' when we really don't want to know.'

'The phrase becomes automatic I suppose,' Sister Joan said thoughtfully, 'but that doesn't detract from the value of the phrase. If you own a valuable painting you might take it for granted but that doesn't detract from the value of the painting … that girl – she looked as if it happened recently – apart from the slight swelling.'

'That's due to adipose tissue, caused by some slight dampness seeping through, from the blankets possibly. We'll know more after the autopsy, but the doctor reckons that she was probably strangled and put in the chest about twenty-five years ago. We shall find out who she is, of course. The adipose tissue only distorts the features very slightly.'

'A local girl?'

They stepped through the front door. The ambulance had gone but there were police cars parked down the side of the building. Through the darkness an occasional police torch flared.

'We'll see.' Bending to open the car door he said, 'I shall press now for an exhumation of Grant Tarquin's body. I think the Sheriff will be more inclined to grant it in view of this latest event, but I must tell you that I'm still pretty certain we'll find Grant Tarquin's body exactly where it's supposed to be. Goodnight, Sister.'

'Goodnight. God bless.'

She stood back as he got behind the wheel and drove away.

'Supper's going to be a few minutes late,' Sister Teresa said, coming out to the front steps. 'I made a winter salad with some grated cheese and soup to start. Do you think the policemen require something?'

'I'll ask. Here's Constable Petrie.' Sister Joan nodded towards the uniformed figure coming round the side of the building.

'This is a bad business, Sister.' The young constable who seemed determined to model himself upon all the slightly bovine policemen found in detective novels of the thirties, greeted them gravely.

'Very unpleasant,' Sister Joan agreed. 'Are you going to be here all night, Constable?'

'Yes, Sister, begging your pardon. Up in the storerooms just to make sure that nothing's disturbed. Not that you good ladies would but there are no security locks on those windows and we don't want anyone nipping in to take away evidence. Not that I think it likely myself. After twenty odd years I doubt there'll be much to find. Oh, there'll be a couple of men patrolling the grounds until the morning too.'

'They'll need to be fed,' Sister Teresa said.

'I think we have all eaten, thank you kindly, Sister,' he said. 'A pot of tea might be very welcome later on though.'

'I'll make some sandwiches and leave them on the kitchen table for you.' Sister Teresa whisked indoors.

'Collect them before I lock up,' Sister Joan said.

'I'll do that, Sister. Thank you.' Constable Petrie paused and added, 'There's talk all these deaths are connected. I think there might be something in that. Only problem is that the first one seems to have happened a long time ago. Same method, different motive, d'ye think?'

'I don't know any longer what to think,' Sister Joan said frankly. 'Constable, do excuse me but I have to go.'

'You go and do what you have to do, Sister,' he returned amiably. 'I'll ask one of the others to give Alice a bit of a walk round the grounds later if that's all right. It'll all help towards her training.'

'Alice's training,' Sister Joan said, amused, 'isn't coming on very fast, but she'll enjoy a walk. Thank you, Constable.'

Supper was different this evening. It simply wasn't possible not to be affected by violence so close at hand even if it wasn't recent violence. The atmosphere was sombre and she read badly, her attention straying from Jeanne d'Arc's visit to the garrison at Vaucouleurs to the unseen but strongly felt presence of the police with their probing torches.

At recreation Mother Dorothy had a word to say.

'As you all know the body of a young girl has been found up in the storerooms. It seems from a preliminary examination that she died at least twenty years ago when this whole estate was in the possession of the Tarquin family, so it is highly unlikely that any of us will have any relevant information to impart since we were not here at that time. If any sister does feel she can contribute some small piece of information, apart from theories, then she must come down to me in the parlour before chapel and if I regard it as pertinent I'll inform Detective Sergeant Mill in the morning so that he can follow up with an interview. When we learn the identity of the poor girl I will of course let you know. Meanwhile there is to be no discussion of this affair among yourselves and you will certainly not talk to any outsiders. The media are bound to descend in force, seeking some sensational revelations which they will very likely invent if they can't find anything. You must therefore keep within doors as much as possible and when you have to go into the grounds wear your veils and keep your eyes firmly on the ground. Sister Joan, your reading tonight lacked a certain liveliness. You described your patron saint's ride to Vaucouleurs as if she was taking a shopping trip to the local supermarket. We must none of us permit these outside events to supersede our first duties to the community.'

'Does anybody know anything relevant?' Sister Gabrielle looked round at the semicircle of silent faces when the prioress had gone. 'No? Right then, let's get on with enjoying the recreation!'

Which was all very fine, Sister Joan thought, as she darned a stocking, but when a particular subject has been forbidden it's amazing how nothing else seems worth talking about!

It was a relief when the bell signalled the end of the period and they could troop down to the chapel. Here the police had been as good as their word. The tactful Constable Petrie was nowhere in evidence and only a rope across the head of the spiral staircase and the locked outer door showed that anything unusual was happening.

Sister Joan went back to the kitchen where three neatly wrapped piles of sandwiches and three small flasks of tea were set. Sister Teresa, since her final profession, was becoming a marvellously practical and obliging laysister. Not to be compared with Sister Margaret, however, who had carried saintliness as easily as a bag of feathers. Sister Joan sighed and smiled as she always did when she thought of Sister Margaret* and putting the food and flasks in a carrier bag set off back to the chapel. She had realized that Constable Petrie, having been instructed to guard the storerooms, wasn't likely to desert his post.

He was in the library, seated at the desk and leafing through a book from which he looked up as she unhooked the rope across the stairs and brought in the snack.

'That's very kind of you, Sister. Oh, sorry, you're not allowed to speak now, are you?' He had lowered his voice respectfully. 'I hope it's all right to look at a book. It's got some views of France in it. The wife and I had our honeymoon there, you know. Very nice but I wasn't too keen on the food. We stayed in Paris and took trips. The Louvre, Napoleon's Tomb, Versailles, Chartres and I don't know what else. There's a lot to see. We went to Reims too, where the statue of Joan of Arc is. Now that would interest you, Sister. Funny, isn't it, to think they burned her up and threw the ashes into the river, and then later on made her a saint and built statues to her? Rather puts you off turning Catholic!'

Sister Joan would have liked to argue but speech being forbidden she merely grinned, shook her head, put sandwiches and flask on the desk and went downstairs again.

A burly policeman whom she didn't recognize barred her way as she crossed the yard, his tone avuncular as he relieved her of the carrier bag.

'This is very kind of you, Sister. I'll see my colleague gets his share. I'll take the dog with me if that's all right with you. Always a good idea to have a dog. Will she come?'

Alice, who had smelt the fish in the sandwiches, had already

* See *Vow of Chastity*

joined them, sitting on her haunches and putting her head on one side with great charm.

'Now you get back inside, Sister, and lock up tight,' he was continuing. 'You can all sleep safe in your beds tonight.'

Sister Joan smiled and went back into the kitchen, wishing that it had been possible to tell the policeman that they all slept soundly most nights without any physical protection save a few locks and bolts which, Detective Sergeant Mill had once observed, could be dealt with by any junior Bill Sykes with an average IQ.

Everything was silent and serene. She checked locks, bolted the door leading from the chapel to the main house, then unbolted it with the reflection that Constable Petrie might appreciate some freedom of movement if anything untoward occurred and certainly wasn't likely to invade the sleeping quarters, and went up to her own cell.

The girl had been strangled about twenty years before. A young girl in a rosebud printed shortie nightie. A girl who might have been reported missing. Sister Joan's last thought as she fell asleep was to wonder where the Tarquins, father and son, had been twenty odd years before.

'Sister, your veil!'

Mother Dorothy stopped her as she came down to chapel in the morning.

'Must we?'

The practice of wearing stifling black veils had largely died out throughout the Order.

'The Press are already here,' Mother Dorothy said in a gloomy tone and pulled down her own veil.

Sister Joan went back to get her veil, irritated by the necessity of having to wear it. The opaque folds of material shadowed the morning and tickled her nose.

Father Malone, looking harassed, arrived and vanished into the sacristy to robe for mass, followed by Sister David. Odd, Sister Joan thought, eyeing the rest of the community, how veils flattened features, slightly distorted outlines, made even little Sister David look mysterious, not quite of the earth.

At breakfast, veils were lifted but the mood was sombre. Father Malone, drinking his coffee, said, 'This is a sad day.

Detective Sergeant Mill was kind enough to call in and tell us what had happened. Poor child! I hope they will find out who she is and then her funeral can be arranged though there are no Catholics gone missing these past years as far as I can recall.'

His tone suggested that going missing was more likely to be a Protestant habit.

'You were parish priest here at that time, weren't you, Father?' Sister Martha asked.

'I was indeed.' He nodded. 'It's over thirty years since I was assigned to this parish you know. Of course I was younger then, a bit of a rebel, so I daresay that the bishop, God rest his soul! considered I'd be better off in a small backwater where they could keep an eye on me.'

'Did you know the Tarquins?' Sister Katherine asked the question that Sister Joan would have put had she not been temporarily diverted by the notion of Father Malone as a rebel.

'Only to pass the time of day with,' Father Malone said. 'They were an old Catholic family long ago but they slid away from the Faith, God help them! and went along with the fashions of the time. Sir Robert was a pleasant enough gentleman, always sent me a very generous contribution for the children's home and the hospital at Christmas. But he travelled a lot. Business, I think. Jewellery and fabrics – various investments. It's my belief that he intended to leave it all to his son, but young Grant was never a credit to him. When he came home which wasn't often he filled the house with his smart friends, and I don't know what else, so Sir Robert used to take off and leave them to it. Maybe he trusted the lad would settle down, but in the end he left nearly everything to charity.'

'And sold the estate very cheaply to our Order,' Sister Joan said.

'Every cloud has a silver lining,' Father Malone said with an air of having just discovered the fact. 'Mind you, as far as I know Grant never broke the law – I mean the law of the land for he broke God's laws many a time, God forgive him! And Sir Robert wasn't a great churchgoer himself at the best of times, but there! he left his son just sufficient to build himself a house and lead a modestly comfortable life and that was all.'

Sister Joan excused herself and went downstairs. In the chapel passage she paused to pull the veil over her face an instant before there was the flash from a long lens camera through one of the windows.

She had thought of it before but it was curious that Sir Robert Tarquin had left his heir so very little. Holding wild parties hardly seemed sufficient reason for someone to be practically disinherited.

The police team was already at work. She stood still in some dismay watching as sacks and boxes were carried down the twisting stairs by men in protective clothing with plastic gloves.

'Good morning, Sister.'

Constable Petrie came down to greet her as she genuflected to the altar.

'Good morning, Constable Petrie. Going off duty?'

'Yes, Sister. Mind you, I dozed off once or twice during the night. All was quiet. I'm afraid the upper storey's out of bounds until the forensics team have finished.'

'There are stacks of old newspapers and documents,' she said. 'I wouldn't want them thrown out with the rubbish.'

'I expect once they've checked and sorted you'll be able to reclaim whatever you want,' he reassured her. 'However I'll have a word.'

'Thank you.'

If she couldn't have a look through everything herself she would have to trust that nothing important went missing. Dissatisfied, she went back into the main house.

'Sister, what shall I do about the menus?' Sister Teresa buttonholed her as she entered the kitchen.

'What menus?' Sister Joan enquired.

'Oh, Sister David found a pile of old menus up in the library – dinner-party menus with lists of house guests from when the Tarquins lived here,' Sister Teresa said. 'She gave them to me when I made my final profession in case I needed any ideas about what to cook for the community, but it was a little joke actually because some of the dinners ran to nine or ten courses.'

'You might as well—' Sister Joan hesitated. 'May I have them, Sister?'

'Yes of course. I just rooted them out of the back of the drawer.' Sister Teresa handed them over.

'Thank you, Sister.'

Sister Joan wandered back into the hall, turning over the handwritten sheets of thin white cardboard with interest. Their whiteness was blurred by ash stains, finger marks, and the occasional cigarette burn, but the handwriting changing down the years from copperplate to a hurried scrawl was only slightly faded and blotted. The menus were dated, and obviously there must have been many more, carefully prepared for the advent of guests, and sometimes kept, she realized, turning a few over at random to read the notes scribbled on the back. 'Lady Sylvia prefers grouse' was one such note. Another informed her that Miss Cecily Blunt took her morning coffee with honey instead of sugar.

Obviously the servants of the day, anxious to be tipped at the end of a country house weekend, had taken care to remember the foibles of individual guests. And the menus! Cream of chicken soup, roast duck with orange sauce and braised celery, poached salmon in aspic with a mustard vinaigrette and fresh strawberries dipped in chocolate with Cornish cream. Her mouth watered. Suddenly a slice of dry bread, a piece of fruit and one cup of coffee seemed a most inadequate breakfast.

'Sister, keeping your eyes lowered doesn't mean you are entitled to walk into walls,' Mother Dorothy said.

Sister Joan was brought up short a few inches away from the front door and muttered a hasty apology.

'You're the one who would have been hurt,' Mother Dorothy said. 'What have you there, Sister?'

'Some old menus and guest lists from the library, Mother Prioress,' Sister Joan said. 'Sister David gave them to Sister Teresa some time ago and Sister Teresa thought she ought to give them to someone.'

'In case the guest lists contain any names useful to the police enquiries? Yes, you had better drive into town, Sister. I imagine Detective Sergeant Mill will be glad to have them,' Mother Dorothy said. 'Oh, here is something for petrol in case you need to fill up the van. We will see you at lunchtime then.'

'Thank you, Mother Dorothy.'

'There is probably sufficient there for you to treat yourself to a cup of coffee as well,' Mother Dorothy said.

'Thank you, Mother Dorothy.' Sister Joan gave her superior a grateful and surprised smile.

'Drive carefully, Sister.' Mother Dorothy gestured to her to pull her veil down properly and went back into the parlour.

It was fortunate that Sister Perpetua and Sister Teresa disliked driving, she thought, since that gave her the opportunity to travel into town more frequently than would otherwise have been the case. She wryly acknowledged it as a fault in herself that from time to time she needed some outside stimulus.

There was no sign of Brother Cuthbert as she passed the former school building. The young monk was probably off meditating somewhere. She wondered if he'd been approached by the media yet, if he even knew that a murder enquiry was in progress. She had driven past a gaggle of reporters with her veil down and her foot hard on the accelerator; now she eased off the speed and put back the veil, relieved to be able to see the world without a dark shadow covering it.

It wasn't strictly according to instructions but she parked the van near the station and, clutching the menus, walked along to the café where she ordered the permitted cup of coffee and began to read through them more carefully.

The early ones dated from the years between the wars when the house had been filled with bright young things who must have played on the tennis court and danced the black bottom and the charleston in what was now the recreation-room. Time was too short to indulge in nostalgic imaginings! She leafed through the pile rapidly, finding several dated during the seventies. The courses were fewer here and only an occasional note on the backs or in the margins gave any clue as to the people who had spent weekends as guests of the Tarquins.

Her eyes fastened suddenly on a note scrawled on the back of a menu dated in the mid-1970s: *Get Mandy a fix. Silly bitch!*

'Skiving off your duties, Sister?' Detective Sergeant Mill had come in and was pulling out a chair.

'How on earth did you know I was here?' she demanded.

'I rang the convent to keep Mother Dorothy up to date on progress and she told me you were coming to see me. I guessed you'd probably be drinking a coffee first while you decided how far to admit me into your investigations,' he said, with an amused tilt of the eyebrow.

'I didn't want to waste your time with the irrelevant,' Sister

Joan said with dignity. 'These are some old menus and guest lists from the years when the Tarquins owned Cornwall House. They were in the back of the kitchen drawer and Sister Teresa thought they might be needed since they came originally from the library. I was looking through them and there's one here I feel you ought to look at.'

She handed over the menu she had just been studying and took the opportunity while his attention was engaged of ordering a coffee for him.

'Thank you, Sister.' He stirred the coffee absently. 'I assume you've got some kind of theory.'

'This looks as if it was a New Year party,' she said eagerly. 'Look, they were going to have salmon and duck and turkey rissoles with braised sprouts. That would be to use up the leftovers from Christmas. I guess the cook was economical. And next to the Toast someone pencilled in "Auld Lang Syne", which is sung at New Year. I think there was a houseparty for the new year of nineteen seventy-five, with guests coming from all over. Sir Robert Tarquin died later that year, didn't he? Probably he was already in poor health and so Grant Tarquin took over most of the preparations and invited some of his own cronies. One was called Mandy and she "needed a fix". That means drugs, doesn't it? Probably there was drugtaking and a quarrel and Grant Tarquin strangled Mandy and stuck her in the old chest. He thought he was going to inherit the estate so he'd dispose of the body later but his father sold it instead, and then even though he visited the house afterwards he never got the chance to move the body, so it stayed where it was all these years.'

'It's a splendid theory,' he said, 'but there's not a shred of proof to support it.'

'There was the body. If you find out who was working at the house when that party was held – oh, it all fits in.'

'There's no proof that Grant Tarquin killed the girl or that her name was Mandy.'

'You have to look for the proof,' she said impatiently. 'Surely if someone called Mandy was reported missing in nineteen seventy-five—'

'From where? There's no central register of missing persons, you know.'

'I would guess London,' she said thoughtfully. 'If she'd been from round here then there would've been more of a fuss about it. Grant Tarquin brought someone from London.'

'Who may or may not have been reported missing.'

'But you'll make enquiries?'

'Yes, Sister. I'll make enquiries at once,' he said. 'No, the coffee's on me. Don't argue. It's not often I get the chance to treat a pretty woman to a cup of coffee. May I have the menus? By the way we have permission to exhume the body of Grant Tarquin. Don't ask me how many strings I had to pull to get that!'

'Will you tell me the results as soon as you know?'

'Of course I'll tell you the results. I have the oddest feeling my life wouldn't be worth living if I didn't,' he said dryly, escorting her into the street. 'Where's your van?'

'In the station yard.'

'I'll walk along with you. You know, Sister, it's going to be the devil of a job trying to find out who did strangle our Jane Doe after all this time. If it was Grant Tarquin—'

'Then he killed Jane Sinclair and Jeb Jones!'

'Twenty years later? Assuming he's still alive, of course.'

'He's alive,' she said tersely. 'I saw him. He's been abroad, Alan; right up to eighteen months ago he hardly ever came back to this country. He couldn't get at the body and he didn't want anyone else to find it either.'

'So?'

'So he heard that the storerooms were going to be cleared out and he had to – no, he couldn't have found out about that until he heard Luther chatting about it in the pub or wherever – he'd already registered with the Falcon Agency.'

'As Mr Monam, I assume?'

'And got his estimate into the filing cabinet in the office at Nightingale Court probably while poor Miss Sinclair had popped out for a minute. You said the lock on the door was very easy to pick.'

'So that she wouldn't meet him face to face? Go on.'

'I can't,' she said ruefully. 'Something made him fear the body was going to be found, and if it wasn't learning about my starting to clear out the storerooms then I don't know what it was.'

'I'll keep in touch, Sister.' He held open the van door for her as she swung herself behind the wheel.

'I'd appreciate that. God bless, Alan.'

'You too,' he said unexpectedly, as she switched on the ignition and drove away.

'Petrol!' She remembered in time just before she turned off on to the moorland track, and pulled into the garage, watching the gauge creep up.

Usually the monthly consumption of petrol was low, since except for the heaviest shopping she rode Lilith into town. Physical life was circumscribed by the rule. It was months since she'd been given permission to spend a day in London to attend an old college reunion.*

And that was when we decided to try to raise money by having retreats for the general public, her mind ran on, as she paid the bill and drove onto the track. We put an advertisement in some of the newspapers, and someone must have read it and assumed that extra space would be required for the guests so there was every chance the trunk would be opened and that poor girl discovered. It must have been a tremendous relief to him when the one retreat didn't lead to any discoveries and proved to be the last, but he must've decided to play safe and get the body out anyway.

He had laid his plans and she had played right into his hands by chatting about clearing out the storerooms. No doubt he'd planned to hire someone – Jeb? – to come and do the actual work. He hadn't reckoned on being checked up on.

Her spirits had leapt up and she speeded past the tall figure of Brother Cuthbert just entering the old schoolhouse without remembering to wave.

---

* See *Vow of Fidelity*

Twelve

New Year, 1975, weekend party at the Tarquin house. Girl named Mandy staying here. Drugs? Was Sir Robert at home at this period? Who were the other guests? Did they know Mandy had been killed? Probably not.

Grant Tarquin – travelled abroad a great deal following his disinheritance. No chance to remove and dispose of body. Did he decide to fake his death so that he could return and make more mischief? He 'died' eighteen months ago before we'd decided on holding weekend retreats. What else was in his mind to do? He kept out of sight when he registered with the Falcon Agency, but Jane Sinclair'd seen him, and linked him with the photographs in the old album that Anne Dalton lent her. Yet when he stood in the yard and looked up at me he didn't try to hide his face. Why? Why did he leave those half prints up in the storerooms? Why was that photograph of – his grandfather? – put inside a roll of old brocade? Was he trying to frighten me? Make me look like a fool when I tried to tell people I'd seen him? Was it to stop me clearing out the storerooms? But if I was stopped someone else in the community would have taken over the job.

Sister Joan stopped writing, read it over, slipped the piece of paper into the back of her diary and rubbed her aching wrist absently. She had already filled up two pages of her spiritual record with an account of her weaknesses and now there was no time left before benediction to work out her theories about Grant Tarquin.

The forensic teams had been up in the storerooms all day, but hadn't interfered with the normal routine of the chapel, since once the bags and smaller boxes had been carried down they had opened, in some cases removed, the upper windows and winched down the larger items. The Press had been banished to the gates where they clustered like pecking hens, cameras and microphones at the ready.

'How I can possibly get the last of the leaves swept and the new compost dug in with people yelling questions at me over the wall I do not know!' Sister Martha said crossly, coming in from the garden as Sister Joan arrived in the hall. 'I was strongly tempted to turn the hosepipe on them if it hadn't seemed too aggressive!'

'They're only doing their job,' Sister Joan said.

'One of them offered me five hundred pounds for letting him take my photograph,' Sister Katherine said, joining them.

'Did you accept?' Sister Joan enquired.

'No, of course not!' Sister Katherine's delicately pretty face flushed. 'It was a great deal of money though. It would've been a tremendous help to the community. If this goes on much longer we shall never get any more postulants and then we'll really be in trouble for the future. Can't you ask your detective sergeant friend to send them all away or something?'

'Sisters, kindly stop chattering and prepare your minds and hearts for chapel,' Mother Dorothy said severely, arriving on the scene in her usual brisk way.

Scolded, they filed into the chapel where Father Malone hovered at the door of the sacristy.

The poetic grace of the benediction washed away other cares. Benediction proper, as opposed to prayers led by Mother Dorothy, was held on Wednesdays and Sundays. Father Malone was taking more than his share of services this week, Sister Joan thought, and suppressed a smile. Father Malone was as keen as anybody else to find out what was going on.

The Angel of the Presence dismissed, they filed out again. Sister Teresa caught up with Sister Joan.

'Do you think they'll have finished soon up in the storerooms?' she asked. 'I don't know whether or not to offer them a meal.'

'Ask Constable Petrie. He's in the kitchen drinking tea this moment,' Sister Perpetua said.

Sister Teresa hurried off.

'I'm glad whenever Father Malone gives benediction.' Sister

Hilaria had drifted up. 'Father Stephens is an estimable young man and recites the litany beautifully but when he elevates the Host I am always conscious of how saintly he looks, whereas when Father Malone does so I see only the Host.'

'I wish I could sum things up as well as you do,' Sister Joan envied. 'You'd make a marvellous detective, Sister, because you go to the heart of the matter. You'd be sure to solve these murders.'

'I heard there'd been murder done.' Sister Hilaria blinked her rather prominent grey eyes and sighed. 'Such a pity that people don't worry about the quality of the life led rather than the manner of the death.'

'But truth is important too, surely!' Sister Joan exclaimed. 'Wrongdoing should be punished.'

'Evil feeds on itself,' Sister Hilaria said tranquilly. 'In the end it eats itself up.'

She went on up the stairs, having said what she intended to say and having shown not the slightest interest in what was going on around her. Or did she simply regard everything from a more rarified point of view?

'Sister, I can't find Alice,' Sister Teresa said, hurrying back along the kitchen corridor. 'I don't want her wandering about with all these reporters at the gate.'

'She wouldn't harm a fly!'

'No, but she'd go off with anyone who offered her a biscuit. I have to help Sister Marie with the serving. Could you—?'

'I'll get Alice, Sister. I'll be eating my supper later than the rest of you anyway since I'm reading.'

'Thank you, Sister. I'm very grateful.' Sister Teresa bustled back again.

Sister Joan pulled down her veil and opened the front door. Outside darkness had fallen but the lights set up by the policemen still up in the storerooms and patrolling the grounds cut through the gloom. It was still unseasonably mild.

'Alice! Alice, here, girl! Good girl!' She raised her voice.

'Your dog's in the stable, Sister – leastways she was five minutes ago,' a constable informed her, materializing from one of the parked cars.

'Thank you, Officer.'

Sister Joan hurried round the corner and headed for the back yard. As she approached the stable Lilith whinnied a greeting and Alice bounded past her, barking.

'Go into the kitchen.' Sister Joan opened the back door and shooed the dog within where she leapt joyfully on Constable Petrie.

Lilith whinnied again.

'One second then,' Sister Joan allowed, hurrying across the cobbles. 'I haven't time to talk to you now.'

Lilith evidently didn't believe her but stretched her neck from her stall and stamped her hooves impatiently.

'It's too late for a walk, girl. Tomorrow I'll take you. Here!'

A basket of carrots stood on the floor, Sister Martha's attempt to wean the ageing pony off sugar lumps. Sister Joan bent to take one and was suddenly jerked backward, something encircling her neck from behind and jack-knifing her until her spine felt ready to snap. Instinctively she flung her hands up to her throat where something was twisting tightly, catching her breath, filling the stable with little dancing stars, drumming the blood in her ears.

She forced herself to go limp and as the grip relaxed for a fraction of a second thrust her fingers between the noose and her skin, drawing one anguished breath that partly cleared her head just as a voice called cheerfully from the yard, 'Are you coming in, Sister? I promised to see everybody safely indoors before I went off duty.'

Constable Petrie had scarcely begun the sentence before the rope or cord was whipped clear and she was thrust so violently against the half door of Lilith's stall that the pony reared back in alarm. Footsteps padded cross the cobbles and were gone.

Her throat was hurting and tears had forced themselves beneath her lids. She twisted about, taking great gulping mouthfuls of air, her hand automatically reaching to soothe the trembling animal.

'Good girl!' Her whisper was hoarse but at least her windpipe didn't appear to be damaged. 'Good girl, easy now.'

Shakily she bent and took out a carrot which Lilith accepted grumblingly. Then she walked unsteadily across to the kitchen.

'Are you all right, Sister?' Constable Petrie had opened the back door.

'Fine,' she got out, grateful for the concealing veil that hid her face and must also have helped to save her life.

'I'll be off then. There'll be a man up in the storeroom area but most of the stuff has gone now. Detective Sergeant Mill is coming over in the morning to have a look round the library but we'll be finished by the weekend. ' 'Night, Sister.'

'God bless.' To her relief her voice came out fairly normally as he passed her.

There was no point in telling anyone yet or in trying to raise the alarm. By now he would be away on to the moor. The unpleasant thought that he seemed to come and go as he chose without being noticed nagged at her nerves. She went to the cupboard and helped herself to a teaspoonful of honey, letting it trickle down her throat. There were no mirrors in the convent but the back of a gleaming copper pan showed dark bruises on her throat just above the round white collar of her habit. She took off her veil and tucked it round her neck, drew several deep breaths and went swiftly along the corridor and up the stairs.

The meal had begun. Heads were bent over the cabbage soup and the dishes of salt cod and steamed vegetables stood on the serving table. Someone – Sister David, she guessed – had put the Jeanne d'Arc typescript on the lectern.

Sister Joan prostrated herself on the floor according to custom for a latecomer and went to the lectern. Her throat ached and despite the honey her voice sounded slightly hoarse.

'During her months at court after the crowning and anointing of the Dauphin, Jeanne indulged her very feminine delight in rich clothes, continuing to dress as a male but wearing the most fashionable doublets with hanging sleeves lined with cloth of gold and silver, silk hose and high boots of calfskin. On her cropped head she sported hats trimmed with coloured feathers and her gloves were lined with silk, but her greatest pleasure lay in the rings her family had given her. She often touched them, turning them about on her fingers, and for her sword she had a scabbard made of white leather lined with scarlet velvet. All the rest of her captain's pay was given to the poor for whom she had great compassion.'

'Sister Joan, you sound as if you're coming down with a cold.' Mother Dorothy had held up her hand to stop the reading. 'Would you like someone to take over the reading?'

'Thank you, Mother Prioress, but I think I'll be all right,' Sister Joan said.

'Very well. Sister Perpetua will give you something for it afterwards. Continue.'

'At that time there was, of course, great poverty in France due to the war and two bad harvests. Jeanne asked for and was granted the remission of all taxes in perpetuity for her own beloved village of Domrémy and the neighbouring village of Greux—'

'Let us give thanks to the Lord for the food we have eaten.' Mother Dorothy recited the brief grace; napkins were folded; the few crumbs on the table swept into a basket for the birds; the rest of the community filed into recreation apart from Sister Hilaria who went out, Bernadette at her heels, to wait for Sister Teresa and Sister Marie; Sister Joan sat down and ate her cold cabbage soup.

The attack, she reasoned, hadn't been a serious attempt to kill her. It had been a warning to her, a warning to back off and not to meddle. Had her attacker really wanted her dead he could have snapped her neck like a twig. She wondered what he had been doing in the stable. Probably playing his old game of 'catch me if you can'. It would have been easy to mingle with the reporters at the front gate, easy to evade the two constables patrolling the extensive grounds.

'Fish, Sister?' Sister Marie had returned and was looking at her enquiringly.

'No, thank you, Sister. I'll go and get something for my throat,' Sister Joan said.

'I'll get Sister Perpetua,' Sister Marie said.

'No, don't trouble her. I know where she keeps the cough linctus,' Sister Joan began, only to be interrupted by Sister Perpetua herself who emerged from the recreation-room as she was speaking.

'You may know where I keep it, Sister, but you're not the infirmarian,' Sister Perpetua scolded. 'Come along. Coltsfoot and honey with a drop of whisky is better than any branded product. They say there's a bug going around. If you want my opinion doctors nowadays call everything a bug to disguise their own ignorance.'

In the cluttered infirmary the dose was measured out, Sister

Perpetua's expression changing as she took a closer look at her younger colleague.

'Tucking a veil into your collar won't remove the bruises any quicker,' she said, gimlet-eyed. 'Has someone tried to strangle you? Or hang you? That's a rope burn.'

'I was attacked just before supper when I went into the stable to see Lilith.'

'You didn't report it?' Sister Perpetua looked disapprovingly.

'I will do so in the morning when Detective Sergeant Mill comes. It wasn't a serious attempt to kill me.'

'Just having a little joke, was he?' Sister Perpetua said grimly. 'What about the rest of us? Is this maniac going to play more jokes on the rest of the community?'

'He'll be gone by now. I think he was hanging around, to test his own nerve as much as anything else, and then he recognized my voice when I spoke to Lilith and – yes, of course! Lilith wasn't whinnying to welcome me! She was greeting her old master! He was always fond of animals, I believe.'

'That will be comforting to remember when someone tries to throttle me,' Sister Perpetua said. 'And who is *he*?'

'Grant Tarquin.'

'Grant Tarquin died, didn't he? I remember hearing something about it last year.'

'He's supposed to have died abroad and his body was brought back and buried in the old cemetery with the rest of his ancestors,' Sister Joan said, 'but I think he's still alive. I'm sure he's still alive.'

'Then who was buried?'

'Not Grant Tarquin,' Sister Joan said. 'Sister, the body in the storeroom has been there for about twenty years, just before Sir Robert died and left the estate away from his son. I think that Grant Tarquin decided to try to get rid of the body. So he—'

'You had better rest your voice,' Sister Perpetua said firmly. 'I assume you've told the police your theory?'

'They have an exhumation order.'

Sister Perpetua gave her a frowning look, shook her head and took a few sips from the whisky bottle she was corking up.

'You had better watch your back, Sister,' she said at last. 'Put a scarf round your throat. It's the usual thing to do when one has a sore throat and there's no sense in alarming the community unnecessarily. Tell Mother Prioress about it in the morning.'

'Yes, Sister.'

Going meekly up to the recreation-room with a short scarf wound about her throat she hoped her superior wouldn't take the alarm and insist on her remaining indoors until the case had been cleared up.

As she came from the blessing as the grand silence began she was amused to see Sister Perpetua waiting for her with a mulish look on her broad, freckled face that dared her to evade her surveillance. Not that she would have done, Sister Joan thought. It was comforting to have someone with her as she stepped across to the stable, to have Sister Perpetua shine her torch into the darkest corners and point with a nod of the head to a length of thin rope lying just inside the door.

Sister Joan picked it up, winding it round her wrist, gave Lilith's velvety nose a stroke and emerged, while Sister Perpetua captured Alice who seemed inclined to go off on patrol again, and walked like a bulky bodyguard at her heels as she went back into the kitchen.

Another thing had become clear. Whoever had cut Lilith's rein in the churchyard and led her away had done so without any apparent trouble. Lilith had a placid nature but she wasn't used to being handled by complete strangers. She had gone quietly then with someone she dimly recognized.

She wished it was possible to discuss recent events with Sister Perpetua, whose practical common sense was a welcome balance to any flights of fancy in which she herself might indulge, but the grand silence was broken only in an emergency. In that silence they went round, turning lights low, checking locks and bolts, returning to the kitchen where Sister Perpetua motioned her to a chair and proceeded to brew a pot of strong tea, giving one cup to Sister Joan and carrying the others through to the chapel wing for the guarding constabulary.

The killer was taking the craziest risks, Sister Joan thought, sipping her tea. To hang round the stable with police on the premises was – why had he come? Had he hoped to slip into the chapel and thence into the main house? She shivered at the picture that conjured up.

Or did he take these risks because, deep down, in that part of him where animals were loved and sanity dwelt, he wanted to be caught?

Sister Perpetua returned and pointed decisively towards the door. There was no point in arguing silently with the infirmarian even if she had felt like it, and she rose obediently and went up the stairs with the older sister looming behind like a very practical guardian angel, got into bed and slept the sleep of utter exhaustion.

Morning had brought the damp mist back, blurring the first streaks of dawn, wafting past the windows like mislaid ectoplasm. Her throat felt better though it was tender to touch. She rose, washed her face, cleaned her teeth, pulled on her habit, tucking the scarf round her neck and draping the dark veil ready to be pulled down if any reporters hove into view. They had apparently balked at spending a night in the open, however, for when she opened the front door and peered through the half dark towards the gates she saw nothing but the grass and the drive and the moor beyond.

A constable, looking dark-chinned and jowly at this early hour, descended from the storerooms and accepted the cup of coffee she had made with alacrity.

'Very nice of you, Sister! All's quiet then. It's my belief that whoever's been doing these murders is miles away by now. You nuns get up early, don't you?'

'Best time of the day!' Sister Joan said brightly, having managed to convince herself of that fact during her novitiate.

'If you say so, Sister.' He gulped his coffee thirstily.

She picked up the wooden rattle which roused the other sisters just as the telephone rang in the kitchen passage.

'Detective Sergeant Mill? Has anything happened?'

She had rushed to pick up the receiver, anticipation speeding her pace. It was very early for a call, which meant that something had happened.

At the other end of the line someone chuckled. Her fingers gripped the receiver more tightly, her heart hammering.

'We have a secret, the Devil and I,' a voice whispered and chuckled again.

Then the phone went dead.

Thirteen

'Sister Joan.' Mother Dorothy detained her as she was leaving the room after breakfast. 'Detective Sergeant Mill rang earlier. Apparently he hasn't time this morning to come up to the convent but requests that you go down to the police station instead. Of course I gave permission. I understand that a member of the forensic team is to have a look round the library so Sister David will escort him there.'

'Thank you, Mother Prioress.' Sister Joan went to put on her cloak and almost bumped into Sister Perpetua.

'And where are you off to now?' the elderly nun demanded.

'I'm driving down to the police station, Sister – and honestly I won't need a bodyguard,' Sister Joan said. 'I'll keep the windows closed and the doors locked and the only person I'll wave to will be Brother Cuthbert, so don't worry.'

She went past swiftly before the other could raise any well-intentioned objections.

The earlier telephone call had shaken her more than she liked to admit. She checked that the doors of the van were locked and the windows wound up before she pulled down her veil and drove out of the yard and round to the front gates where a large policeman was chatting to a group of reporters. Cameras flashed as she speeded past, foot hard down, tiptilted profile unyielding behind the concealing veil. The one thing dreaded in any convent was unwelcome publicity. It was the one thing she had always been very careful to avoid when helping out the police in previous cases.

Detective Sergeant Mill was at his desk, a certain suppressed excitement in his manner as he rose and nodded towards a chair.

'Good of you to come so quickly, Sister,' he said. 'Would you like some coffee?'

'Please.' She had lifted her veil and saw his dark eyes move to the scarf at her throat.

'Not the flu that's going round, I hope?' he said.

'No. I'll tell you about that later,' she said. 'Mother Dorothy said you wished to see me.'

'We exhumed the body of Grant Tarquin last evening,' he said.

'And?'

'You were right, Sister. The body buried under that name was facially disfigured due, apparently, to injuries sustained during the fatal car accident. It is, however, the body of a man in his early sixties with greying hair, certainly not the remains of Grant Tarquin.'

'The doctor who signed the death certificate and then went off somewhere?'

'Further enquiries will have to be made, of course, but I'm certain we'll find that Dr Gullegein never practised any medicine after he left Turkey. Whether his death was an accident or not we don't yet know. My own opinion is that Grant Tarquin killed him, staged the car accident in some remote part of Turkey where neither of them was known and made the exchange of identities. Then Grant Tarquin simply slipped over the nearest border and travelled for over a year while Dr Gullegein was being buried over here in the old cemetery.'

'He decided to come back having been declared dead. To get the body of the young girl in the storeroom?'

'Yes.'

'But why now? After twenty years?' she exclaimed.

'Let's reconstruct a possible scenario,' Detective Sergeant Mill said. 'During a New Year party a young girl is killed. My own belief is that the other members of the houseparty were unaware of what had happened. Grant Tarquin might have told them she'd left early. Incidentally Sir Robert Tarquin, according to the hospital records, was being operated on for varicose veins at the time. So he wasn't present. Grant Tarquin hid the girl's body in the trunk meaning to dispose of it later, since he was under the impression that he was going to inherit the estate anyway. With other guests present it was probably too risky to try to dispose of it at the time. Then his father dies suddenly, leaving him only a competence, and the estate is sold cheaply to your Order. You know that Grant Tarquin was married as a young man?'

'His wife and child died in a car crash,' Sister Joan nodded. 'I've often wondered if his evil nature wasn't the result of a twisted grief.'

'He was always wild,' Detective Sergeant Mill said, 'but after that he became quite unconcerned about his behaviour. So, there he is, disinherited, unable to get into the storerooms even though he cultivated friendship with the sisters here at that time.'

'A perverted kind of friendship,' Sister Joan said disapprovingly.*

'Morally so, but not against the law of the land,' he agreed. 'Then he goes abroad, knowing that though in the past he's been welcome at the convent that welcome didn't extend to his having a free run of the storerooms. Better to leave things as they were, but always the possibility of something being discovered must have preyed on his mind. And then, when the pressure threatens to become overwhelming, he meets the good Dr Gullegein, out in Turkey. Here's a chance to change his identity, to officially die, and later to return to the district and make arrangements to remove that trunk.'

'Then he must've killed the doctor,' Sister Joan said.

'Apparently Gullegein had no relatives, no close friends. He lived up country – I understand he was a fairly heavy drinker. Grant Tarquin spins him some yarn about needing to be pronounced dead – maybe he tells him he's involved in drugs – the good doctor signs the necessary papers; they get drunk together or rather Gullegein does. Tarquin tells his friend he'll drive him home, stages the accident, represents himself as the doctor to the local police, produces the death certificate, swaps his own photo for the doctor's in the passport – it's possible they'd already done that – and quietly leaves the country. A bit of quick talking, maybe a judicious bribe to the police chief so that awkward questions won't be asked— What puzzles me is

* See *Vow of Silence*

why the devil he took the risk of coming back here and trying to get hold of that trunk anyway. Even if it'd been found, he was officially dead. There was nothing to connect him with a murder that was twenty years old!'

'I think it was the enormity of the risk that appealed to him,' Sister Joan said thoughtfully. 'He'd always taken risks. It can become a compulsion – to go on and on, and in the end to start thinking you're invulnerable. But he must've been blown out with conceit. Staying in his own house near the old town hall?'

'I expect we'll find that he came into the country with a crowd of other tourists waving his own passport for a cursory inspection. The controls at borders are much more lax than they used to be. He hires a car, fills it with supplies bought in the safe anonymity of London and drives to the house, only to find young Jeb Jones installed there as a squatter, which is a circumstance he turns to advantage. Jeb isn't a local lad. He can easily be bribed to keep quiet about Grant Tarquin's presence in the house. He lies low, registering by telephone with the Falcon Agency as Mr Monam, scrap merchant and silversmith, sneaks into the office in Nightingale Court to put his estimate in the filing cabinet, prints out the so-called circular, offering his services in clearing out the convent – by the way I doubt if he even knew that you'd started the spring-cleaning. He couldn't have risked going into any of the local pubs where Luther was chattering for fear of being recognized. If you'd taken him up on his offer it's my belief he'd have sent Jeb and perhaps a couple more out-of-towners to carry out the actual removals. The chest was closed, if you recall—'

'A secret spring,' Sister Joan nodded, her eyes intent on his face.

'Go on yourself, Sister,' he invited. 'The rest of the scenario is yours.'

'I've been thinking that he probably sent Jeb over to tiptoe round the storerooms and check up on the amount of stuff to be moved. Grant Tarquin wouldn't know exactly how much had been added in the past few years. I'd found the photograph of Sir Richard Tarquin—'

'Wild Devil Tarquin,' Detective Sergeant Mill nodded. 'The old boy left quite a reputation behind him. Tales of pacts with the Devil and the Lord knows what else!'

'I know that Grant Tarquin liked to model himself on his grandfather,' Sister Joan said. 'Probably he had that photograph in his possession already and told Jeb to hide it in the roll of brocade.'

'Why?'

'To scare off anybody who might start rooting about among the rubbish?' she suggested. 'If you've an attic full of rubbish and a chance to have someone take it away, it would be very natural to go up and have a quick look round in case there was anything there you might want to keep. A sister coming across the photograph with that inscription on the back would have decided to get rid of the lot without further investigation.'

'But not this sister?'

'Not this sister,' she agreed.

The desk sergeant brought coffee. She sipped hers, feeling its warmth trickle down her throat, easing the soreness.

'And the footprints?' he asked.

'I think now that was merely Jeb tiptoeing around,' she said consideringly. 'It was Sister David who reminded me that devil worshippers are reputed to tiptoe in sacred places. There were half footprints in the chapel of rest in the old cemetery too. Would that have been Jeb getting too curious for his own good?'

'I don't know why we don't enrol you in the CID, Sister,' he said, looking amused. 'You're quite right, of course. We compared the prints in the chapel of rest with the shoes Jeb was wearing and they matched. My own guess is that Grant Tarquin went out at night for exercise and popped into the chapel to avoid being spotted. Probably young Jeb saw him coming out of the chapel and popped in himself out of curiosity.'

'And was killed later on back at the house.' She shivered.

'Now, suppose you tell me what happened to you in the stable last night.'

'Someone rang you?'

'Sister Perpetua. She feared you might let it "slip your mind". What went on, Sister Joan?'

She told him briefly; unwillingly, at his command, pulling aside the scarf to show the bruises.

'We've an all points alert out for him,' he said, 'and an appeal on the TV for anyone with information to come forward. Don't be too hard on the media. They have their uses. He can't hide out for ever.'

'Isn't a cornered man more dangerous, more likely to take risks?' she hazarded.

'We'll find him. Meanwhile—' He rose.

'Don't go out in the dark alone.'

'Don't go *anywhere* alone. Do you want an escort back to the convent?'

'I'll drive straight back without stopping,' she promised.

'We're still trying to identify the young girl,' he said, moving to the door. 'No luck in that department yet. Of course she might never have been reported missing. Take care, Joan.'

'You too. God bless.' She nodded towards the desk sergeant and went out to the car.

Father Malone was coming along the street, a battered briefcase under his arm, his expression hurried.

'Sister Joan, I didn't get the chance of a word this morning.' He paused with his short legs poised for flight upon whatever errand of mercy he was bound. 'Is your sore throat better? So many down with it! Happily Brother Cuthbert is recovering under Sister Jerome's care. She has proved a first-class housekeeper even if her nature is a trifle dour, poor soul, but she won't let him out of bed yet! Do you think they will clear up this bad business quickly? Advent is a preparation for the birth of our Blessed Lord, after all.'

'I think they're making progress, Father.'

'We live in violent times, Sister. Take care now.' He patted her shoulder and wandered on.

'Home, James!' Sister Joan patted the wheel of the van and leaned forward to turn the ignition key.

Her next duty was to inform Mother Dorothy of the attack on her. Her lips curved in a wry grin as she privately acknowledged Sister Perpetua's sophistry. The older nun had kept her promise to say nothing to the prioress but had made sure the police knew.

The sun was struggling to emerge through a light drizzle of rain that had started, turning the surrounding landscape into a shimmering mist of golden drops. There was water in the deep ruts along the track and she steered an erratic course to avoid them.

'Oh, no! Silly man!'

Brother Cuthbert, seemingly oblivious to the weather, was fiddling inside the engine of the old car parked at the side of the little schoolhouse for all the world as if he wasn't supposed to be in bed with a sore throat.

She slammed on the brakes, undid her seat belt and climbed down, her low heels sinking into the wet grass. When Brother Cuthbert was working on the car he wouldn't have heard Gabriel's trumpet.

'Brother Cuthbert, what on earth are you doing out of b—?'

But the young monk wouldn't be in bed in the makeshift hermitage into which the little schoolhouse had been adapted. Sister Jerome wouldn't have trailed on foot up here every day to nurse him. Brother Cuthbert had been ordered down to the Presbytery to tend his sore throat. That must have been what he was mouthing at her when she'd driven past a couple of days ago.

She turned to flee, the grass making a squelching noise as she pulled up her foot, and in that second the tall, cowled figure straightened up, turned, and strode towards her, gripping her arm as her hand grasped the van door handle.

'You shouldn't have got out of the van, Sister,' Grant Tarquin said.

'You've been here since—'

'Since the monk packed his bag and went off into town with Father Malone. He was coughing badly so I reckoned he'd be gone for a couple of days. There was food inside so I didn't have to go shopping. Young Jeb used to do most of it. He was really quite useful in that way.'

It was astonishing, she thought through her terror, how even now, even here, his charm was palpable. The brilliantly cold dark eyes, the sensual mouth and deep pleasant voice hadn't changed since her last brief acquaintanceship with him.

'Now it's impossible for me to go shopping with the media prying into every nook and cranny,' he was continuing. 'And I can hardly go and rent a car or get on the nearest train, so I've been looking at the old banger over there, hoping to get it going again. It was risky but I've always loved a risk and there was a spare habit inside, so I took the chance. Now don't go saying that I'll never get away with it. I've managed very nicely so far.'

'I was going to ask you to let go of my arm,' Sister Joan said. 'You've given me too many bruises already.'

'Last night? Sorry about that.' He had loosed his grip and she sat down shakily on the top step of the van. 'It suddenly occurred to me that I might use Lilith for a getaway, but the dog came bounding in to greet me – nice little animal by the bye – and then I heard your voice. I wasn't going to kill you, Sister. I only kill when it's absolutely necessary.'

'Was it necessary to kill that poor girl in the trunk?' she demanded.

'Poor girl? Oh, Mandy! I never knew her second name.' He smiled, his teeth very white against the darkness of his face. 'She was a bit of a tart from London I picked up. I thought it might be amusing to *pass her off as a lady!*'

He had emphasized the last words with a contempt that made her feel suddenly more frightened than before. Here was someone who simply didn't consider other people as anything other than objects to be used and abused as he thought fit.

'You killed her,' she said.

'The silly bitch wanted something stronger than hash, and I lost my temper. We were up in the storeroom. The trunk was there.'

'Nobody missed her?'

'Not as far as I ever heard.' He shrugged slightly. 'I told the other guests she'd been called home – look, I didn't mean to hurt her but I had to shut her up, don't you understand? I wasn't myself at the time. My wife had died the previous year and I – so I went a bit wild. If my father hadn't been such a wretched old Puritan maybe things would've been different. I'd have moved the girl's body the minute the rest of the crowd had gone, but I wait sometimes too long before I act. There's excitement in that, like playing chicken on a motorway. Then my father died and the estate was left to be sold to your precious sisterhood, and after that I never had the opportunity to spend a long, uninterrupted time up in the storerooms. Even if I'd unearthed the trunk how the devil could I have got the body down the stairs with nuns in and out of the chapel all the time? Finally I went abroad but that trunk stayed at the bottom of my mind like a burr under a horse's saddle and I knew that sooner or later I'd have to do something about it so I hit on the notion of being declared dead.'

'So you killed the doctor. How could you?'

'Because he was a fool,' Grant Tarquin said coldly. 'I asked him for a death certificate, told him it was a joke I was planning to play on some friends. He agreed – for a consideration and then after he'd done it he wanted more. We were up in the high country on a driving trip at the time. I lost my temper and hit him. Then it occurred to me that I'd better get rid of him, so I pushed him into the car before he regained consciousness and sent it over a cliff. It was an unfortunate necessity. Then I waited for over a year – travelled about a bit and finally slipped back into the country.'

'And registered with the Falcon Agency. We know the rest.'

'Of course I had to lie low. I did everything by telephone. And finding Jeb in my house was a bonus. Jeb would do anything in return for a roof over his head.'

'I'm sure he would,' Sister Joan said, 'but I daresay he'd draw the line at murder?'

'I told him that I wanted to leave something up in the storeroom to scare the sisters. I'd had that photograph for years. It looks just like me, don't you think? We have a secret the Devil and I. That used to be the old Tarquin motto, you know, back in the fifteenth century when Sir Richard went off to serve the Earl of Warwick. Of course he wasn't knighted then. That came later, for special services rendered, along with the motto. But that was a very long time ago.'

'You killed Jane Sinclair. That was no accident.'

'The silly wench liked wandering about in the cemetery, reading the inscriptions on the tombstones. I had to dodge her several times when I was out for an evening stroll. Then one evening I looked up and there she was, standing at a window, staring at me. Staring as if she recognized me.'

'She saw some photographs of your father and grandfather in an old album.'

'So she told me. I rang her up, asked her to come along to her office because I wanted to make a few enquiries about her landlady and she came. If she hadn't said anything she'd have been fine but she stood up, looked at me, and said, "But I thought Grant Tarquin was dead". Silly girl!'

'And then you killed Jeb Jones.'

'He sneaked into the convent without my leave. Going to find out what he could steal I daresay. Some old biddy gave him a crack across the nose with her walking stick so he ran away. He said he was going back there. I couldn't have that.'

'In other words you kill anyone who might get in your way.'

'Including you, Sister. You keep hoping that while we're chatting someone will come by. Nobody will, you know. It's raining quite hard now – not the weather for a walk. Even the mass media is no longer gathering in such force. Sorry, Sister Joan!'

'Not as sorry as I am,' she said with feeling.

'You know I do regret not having got to know you better,' he said with a chuckle. 'When we met before* it was only briefly and your interfering stopped me from amusing myself. It seems you have a certain amount of spunk. Wasted in a convent, of course.'

'Not entirely,' Sister Joan said, and launched herself at him like a small fury, trusting in the element of surprise that might throw him off balance and give her the vital few seconds she needed in order to climb into the van and lock the door.

It was fruitless, of course. He staggered for a moment, then recovered his balance, his hands reaching to fasten on her throat where the scarf protected her. There was a drumming in her ears, a roaring noise that came from somewhere beyond the rain and the sound of a siren, at that instant more blessed than bells. He had dragged her sideways, and his cowl had fallen from his black head where the hair was plastered by the rain to his temples. The world tilted and blurred and then she was flung violently aside and, as she gasped for breath, the van began to move.

'Look out!' She thought she had yelled and then realized her voice had emerged as a whisper.

The van struck him in the back, gained speed as it ran down a slope between the deep puddles and tipped sideways. She had a glimpse of his back arched against the weight and then he went down under the wheels and there was silence again.

'Sister, are you all right?'

Constable Petrie ran to her, helping her to her feet.

---

* See *Vow of Silence*

'I'm fine,' she said shiveringly.

'Sister Perpetua telephoned the station. You'd said something about stopping off to chat to Brother Cuthbert and she recalled that he was down at the Presbytery recovering from a cold. Father Malone didn't tell us that so we didn't search the school.'

'Grant Tarquin—'

'Won't be killing anyone else,' Constable Petrie said grimly.

'I know I put the brake on. I know I did.'

'That's an old van, Sister. He threw you hard against the side and the vibration probably set something off. The ground's pretty treacherous just here too. Sister Joan's all right, sir.'

He broke off to address Detective Sergeant Mill who strode up.

'Sister Joan has ninety-nine lives,' Detective Sergeant Mill said. 'It only bothers me that she's using them up so fast.'

''It was—'

'A freak accident, Sister. You can't blame yourself. A blessing in a way. He'd have been declared insane. Come on!'

She allowed herself to be guided towards the police car.

'Killing was becoming a habit with him.' He leaned to fasten her seat belt. 'Take a few deep breaths and put your veil down. We'll be overrun with reporters and photographers before you know it.'

'Lord forbid!' She tugged at her veil.

'I'll run you back to the convent and explain the whole affair to Mother Prioress. At least this way there won't be a trial.'

'There'll have to be a funeral.'

'And this time he'll stay buried,' the detective said. 'Don't waste any pity on him, Sister. He was bad – genes, I daresay.'

But that excused everybody from personal responsibility, she thought. Tendencies were implicit in everybody but there were other things like conscience and duty and – she'd argue about it later. All she wanted to do now was lean her head against the back of the seat, close her eyes and allow herself to be driven unresistingly home.

Fourteen

'At least the reporters have gone,' Mother Dorothy said with some satisfaction in her tone. 'No doubt the headlines will inform the public that the murderer cheated justice, and I am very pleased that we don't have to read them. It will be a nine day wonder.

'He was a very wicked man,' Sister Gabrielle said, 'and I for one am delighted that he was the last of his line.'

'Old families are often inbred,' Sister Mary Concepta murmured in her gentle way.

'You'd find excuses for the Devil himself,' Sister Perpetua said.

'Rather less talk of the Devil ought to be our resolution from now on,' Mother Dorothy said severely. 'I've asked Father Malone to come in and hold a short service of consecration in the storerooms and the sooner we return to normality the better.'

'Meaning poor,' Sister Perpetua remarked darkly.

'There was nothing of great value amid all the rubbish.' Mother Dorothy's voice held a shade of regret. 'We shall make a couple of hundred from the Victorian artefacts that Sister Joan brought down, but that's it, I'm afraid.'

'Then what are we going to do, Mother?' Sister Katherine looked up anxiously from her needlework.

'We generally contrive to manage,' Mother Dorothy said. 'We are after all vowed to poverty. Perhaps we require to be reminded of that from time to time. However there are many others worse off than we are. Neither is the news all bad. Sister Katherine has just received an order for lace for first communion veils which will bring in a nice little sum. Sister

Joan will be glad to help her with it.'

'Making lace?' Sister Joan looked alarmed. 'I never—'

'Hemming and a little embroidery to put the finishing touches,' the Prioress said. 'And your own talent for painting can be utilized. We can sell calendars and mass cards. Easter cards too. We're too near Christmas to get cards for that festival out in time, but we might make quite a decent amount by and by. However that's for next year. We must redouble our prayers and increase our economies and trust all will be well. We can certainly economize a little more. The diet has become positively gourmet recently. Soup and sandwiches at lunchtime are quite unnecessary. Soup with a slice of bread and a piece of fruit will keep us all beautifully slim. We shall be in the fashion. Oh, it will be necessary to ride Lilith into town from now on. Detective Sergeant Mill kindly offered to sell the van for us since I doubt if anyone will wish to drive it again. Too potent a reminder of a most unfortunate accident.'

'Not so unfortunate!' Sister Gabrielle protested. 'That wretch meant to kill Sister Joan. It's my belief that it was the Blessed Michael himself who jerked those brakes into action.'

'Well, that's a matter of opinion.' Mother Dorothy looked as if she refrained from argument with an effort. 'We shall go to our work now, Sisters, with renewed zeal. Sister Joan, yesterday's events must have shaken you considerably, so you must take things easily.'

'Thank you, Mother, but I feel perfectly all right,' Sister Joan said. 'I've one or two small jobs to do and they'll take my mind off recent happenings.'

Actually now that the storerooms had been cleared and swept by the police there was a feeling of time hanging heavily on her hands.

She wandered out into the yard with some notion of grooming Lilith and almost walked into Constable Petrie who was coming round the corner with Alice leaping at his heels.

'I'm surprised to see you up and about, Sister,' he said. 'You ought to be putting your feet up after such a nasty experience, you know. Oh, the boss sends regards. He's busy with all the paperwork so we can get this whole business finished with for good. I came over to flush out the last of the reporters and give Alice a bit of training.'

'That's very kind of you, Sergeant.'

'Constable, Sister.' His pink complexion had flushed. 'Sergeant would be nice.'

'As far as I'm concerned you're already promoted,' Sister Joan said.

'That's very kind of you, Sister. Well, I'd best get on.' He saluted smartly. 'All right and tight! But you ought to think about getting a few extra locks round this place. On the stable, for example.'

'Locks.' She repeated the word and favoured him with a sudden broad and brilliant smile. 'Thank you! I've just remembered a task I simply can't postpone any longer.'

'I'll leave you to it then, Sister.' He saluted again, said, 'My, Sergeant Petrie' as if he were practising for promotion and went off jauntily.

The box of tools and odd bits of metal was still in the stable. She pulled it out and found the rusted bolt. Sister David would be pleased to be able to lock up her precious books. It was a pity none of them had been revealed as a valuable first edition.

One of the curtain rings leapt up and fell back as the remaining objects in the box settled. She reached in and picked it up, slipping in on to her finger. It was very small for a curtain ring. Very thick too. She hesitated, then burrowed for its fellow which was of equal size and weight.

'I'll get these cleaned up.' She rose and went indoors again.

An hour later she wiped the last trace of encrusted dirt from the second ring and held them up to the feeble sunlight that filtered through the window. Her heart was beating rapidly.

'Are you all right, Sister?' Mother Dorothy, doing her afternoon rounds, had paused at the kitchen door.

'Mother, do we have a magnifying glass?' Sister Joan asked.

'I have one in the parlour. You'd better come and use it.' Without asking for further clarification the prioress led the way down the kitchen passage.

'Dominus vobiscum.' She took a round magnifying glass from her desk drawer and motioned to Sister Joan to take a seat.

'Et cum spiritu tuo. Mother Dorothy, do you believe in miracles?'

'Of all the foolish questions you've ever asked that one must take the palm,' Mother Dorothy said, amused. 'What have you there?'

'I thought they were curtain rings, but they're finger rings,' Sister Joan said. 'Gold too. But it's more than that! Mother, look at the inscriptions on the outer rims. You can feel them with the tip of your finger but you need the glass to read them.'

Mother Dorothy took one of the rings, fixed the glass at a suitable distance from it and peered closely.

'IESU,' she spelled slowly. 'Jesu in modern Latin.'

'And on the other is MARIA,' Sister Joan said eagerly. 'Don't you see?'

'No.' Mother Dorothy laid down the rings and the magnifying glass and looked at her.

'In fourteen hundred and thirty-one Sir Richard Tarquine who wasn't yet a "sir" because he hadn't been knighted served in France during the Hundred Years' War. He served under the Earl of Warwick who knighted him during that campaign, "for services rendered". Warwick was in charge of the English garrisons when Jeanne d'Arc was imprisoned at Rouen. Her rings were taken away from her – the two rings her family had given her – one inscribed with the name of Jesu and the other with the name of Maria. She used to touch the rings before she went into battle and some people thought they had magical powers.'

'You surely don't imagine – my dear girl, that's simply not—' Mother Dorothy broke off, staring at her.

'She was guarded by five soldiers turn and turn about. They teased and harassed her but they never did her physical injury. They feared her because they thought she was a witch, a child of the Devil. Suppose one of them took her rings away, hoping to use their magical powers for his own ends? Suppose his name was Richard Tarquine? Mother Dorothy, think of that ancient motto of the Tarquin family! "We have a secret, the Devil and I". Could this be it? Everything she was – her ashes and her heart – everything she owned was said to have been broken up and thrown into the river. There are no relics of Jeanne d'Arc.'

'And these rings could be the ones she loved because her family had given them to her? There would be no way of telling.'

'But we know Richard Tarquine served the Earl of Warwick at the right time and was knighted and given the motto for unspecified services. For guarding Jeanne d'Arc, perhaps? Warwick wouldn't have known where the rings had gone. Nobody seems to have known.'

'The only known relics of Jeanne d'Arc?' Mother Dorothy picked up the magnifying glass and studied the rings again. 'That would certainly increase vocations.'

'Would we be allowed to keep them?'

'I have no idea.' Mother Dorothy sighed. 'The bishop might know. Since they were stolen from her in the first place then they could be regarded as the spoils of war. Surely there'd be a tradition in the family.'

'The Tarquins changed their religion according to the political climate of the times,' Sister Joan argued. 'The old Catholicism was laid aside during the sixteenth century when the Tudor Elizabeth came to the throne. The rings were put away, lost, forgotten. Only the motto and some vague story of pacts with the Devil remained. Maybe the original Richard Tarquine vowed his soul to the Devil on the rings in return for riches and prosperity.'

'And six hundred years later the Devil came to claim his forfeit? You have a romantic imagination, Sister!'

'Mother, haven't we been praying for extra income for ages?' Sister Joan said.

'And if these rings do date back to the fifteenth century then the possibility of their being genuine is vastly increased,' her superior nodded. 'Vocations would increase; visitors would come to look at them on display; the media would photograph them, feature them in some arts programme on television – it would create a great stir.'

Her voice and face were suddenly sombre.

'What do you want me to do?' Sister Joan asked.

'Weigh everything up,' Mother Dorothy said slowly, 'then do what your heart bids. You've a good heart and you're not completely devoid of common sense either. Do what your heart tells you. Take them with you, and think. Try thinking, Sister. *Dominus vobiscum.*'

'*Et cum spiritu sancto.*' Sister Joan picked up the hollow, shining circles and bent her knee.

In the garden the ground was still wet, the bare bushes spangled with raindrops. The moor beyond the open gates was deserted, cameras and prying questions swept away. Behind her the peaceful façade of the old house belied the quiet activity of its occupants.

Soup and no sandwiches for lunch. Sewing hems for Sister Katherine. Painting sentimental little pictures to be sold as cards and calendars. Poverty freely chosen and embraced with love. She sighed and shook her head.

Detective Sergeant Mill drew up and opened the car door. He was taking a roundabout way to the convent and ought to be stepping on the gas if he planned to arrive before the sisters filed into chapel but a few minutes' pause wouldn't hurt. It was refreshing after the long hours filling out forms, poring over coroners' reports, to steal a few minutes for himself, to contemplate with pleasure the high, wild ground, interrupted by deep pools and long, meandering streams swollen by the recent rains that met and merged and headed for the river and thence to the sea.

The rest of the lads at the station had contributed generously to the whipround. There was sufficient to buy the neat little secondhand van he'd had his eye on for some time. He'd had a word with the garage owner and the sisters'd be getting their petrol half price in future. He could easily scrape up the extra out of his salary.

He stretched his long legs, leaned against the side of the car and lit one of the occasional cigarettes he allowed himself. On the horizon a cloaked figure rode into view, heading towards the river. Anyone else would be taking it easy, he thought with impatient tenderness but no! there she went, exercising that old pony. Not even turning her head in his direction! He lifted an arm, then lowered it again. Their official business together was done and he had Mother Dorothy to see.

The moor sloped down to where three streams conjoined to flow down to the river. Sister Joan dismounted and stood, Lilith's rein loose in her hand. Everything Jeanne had ever owned had been seen, fingered, investigated and stolen. Even her bones had been pounded into ashes. It could all happen again – the experts arguing, the reporters and the cameramen with their questions, the young girls flocking to the postulancy for the wrong reasons.

She walked slowly to the deep hollow where the three streams gushed together and ran swiftly down to the river curving through the valley far below. The two rings in her hand felt warm and heavy.

'Have them back now, Jeanne love,' she said softly and let them fall and be carried downriver, flashing briefly on the surface of the bubbling water before they vanished from sight.

Time to get that lock fixed and then see what Sister Katherine needed doing. She remounted, gathered up the reins and decided as she turned the pony's head homeward that the religious life was for the terminally eccentric.

'Never mind!' she said aloud, leaning to give Lilith a pat. 'When I'm allowed pocket money again I'll buy a lottery ticket. There's no rule against that and you never know your luck, old girl! You never know your luck!'

)